MW00789449

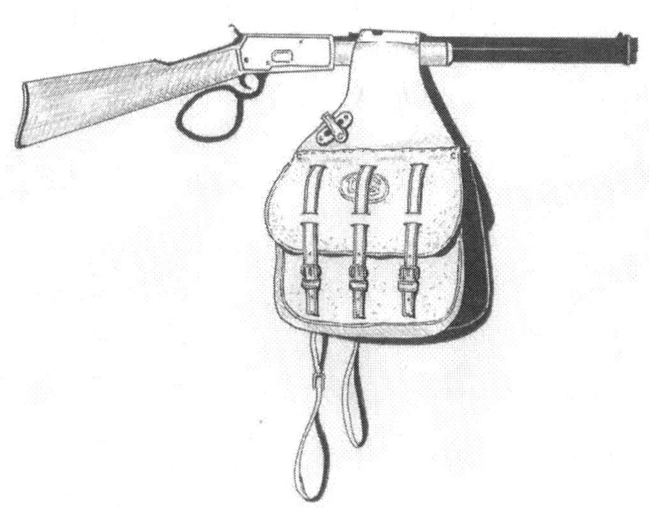

Look for other Adventure & Western novels
by
Eric H. Heisner

West to Bravo

T. H. Elkman

Short Western Tales: Friend of the Devil

Africa Tusk

Wings of the Pirate

Follow book releases and film productions at:
www.leandogproductions.com

Seven Fingers a' Brazos

Eric H. Heisner

Illustrations by Al P. Bringas

Visit our website at
www.leandogproductions.com

Illustrations by: Al P. Bringas
Contact: al_bringas@yahoo.com

Dustcover jacket design: Clint A. Beach
Contact info: Thebeachboy72@gmail.com

Paperback ISBN: 978-0-9995602-3-5

Printed in the United States of America

Dedication

For Augie

Special Thanks

Amber W. Heisner,
Clint Beach,
Al P. Bringas
& Bruce Boxleitner

Note from Author

Before my first Western novel was published, I knew that I had to pick a story with enduring characters. From years of experience, the key to writing was in the rewriting. *West to Bravo* hit the presses in 2014, successfully selling worldwide, proving to be a story that resonates well with fans of the traditional Western genre.

The personalities that came to life through a conglomeration of classic western images has stuck with me and steeped itself into another story to be told. Familiar faces return in this new adventure in fiction. The demands of manhood and family are put to the test.

The American West and what it represents has shaped the world and how we as a nation are perceived. Self-reliance, moral integrity and the independent spirit are ideals that have also guided me as a storyteller. We hear the term 'political correctness' in today's society which sometimes translates to, a fear to tell the truth.

Western stories portray who we are as imperfect and evolving beings along with the consequences of a developing civilization on the frontier. We will forever be on the horizon of newness in society. Historical tales reflect the basic human characteristics that drive us and help to serve as a guide on this path of survival.

Eric H. Heisner

August 14th, 2018

The adventure from **West to Bravo**
continues …

The crackle of flames on a burning wagon and the sharp snapping report of firearms put feelings of dread to the lower bowels. A four-up mule team is cut away from a wheeled cart with fiery canvas flapping loose in the breeze on wooden ribs. Fear-struck men scurry in an outbreak of desperation. Several horseback bandits swerve in and out of the wagon circle with pistols and rifles discharging in all directions. The devastating band of marauders methodically shoots down every moving being in unrepentant butchery.

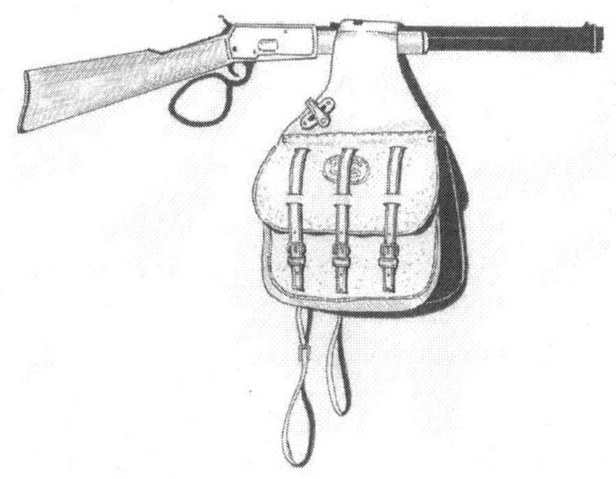

Chapter 1

On the high plateaus of north-central Arizona, several wagons with panicked teams of animals, mostly still hitched, are assembled in a broken defensive circle. The dark smoke from burning supplies mixed with the acrid smell of expelled gun-powder fills the camp and hangs in the thick surrounding pines. Fleeing men dash for the surrounding cover of vegetation and are shot down without mercy in the brutal assault. Horrific screams of agony from man, woman and child echo through the empty land in testimony to the ferocity of the attack.

The smell of fire, the ear-splitting sounds of gunshots and wisps of eye-burning smoke surround a young boy inside a covered wagon. He huddles close with his protective mother and two older sisters. They sit deep in the wagon bed surrounded by the life subsidizing gear stowed for the big move west. They all watch, apprehensive, as the horseback riders' shadows pass the buttoned down canvas covering while the mother clutches the girls tighter.

The boy holds a large-framed Walker horse pistol with the hammer pulled back and ready. He aims the long, nine-inch barreled firearm, propped over a quilted sack, at the small rear opening of the canvas topper. With his jaw clenched taut and lips quivering from fright, the boy sits, determined to defend his family.

The dying sounds of screaming horses and yelling menfolk cause the small cluster of family inside the wagon to shudder. The young girls sob quietly, as their mother closes her eyes firm in silent prayer. Eventually, sounds of the vicious fighting fade and leave only the heavy breathing snorts of horses, mounted hooves on rocky ground and the scuffle of men's boots circling the battleground. The boy looks to his mother and sisters, then back at the long-barreled pistol in his sweaty, trembling palms.

Suddenly, the canvas cover of the wagon is pulled back from the wooden support ribs overhead. A gruff bearded man cuts the secured tethers with an antler handled knife and yanks the tarpaulin to the ground. He eyes the sundries and looks, with surprise, at the clustered family hidden inside the homesteader wagon.

For a long, heart-stopping moment he stares, with an evil glint at the mother and sobbing girls. His gaze then travels over to the boy, not yet in his teens. He gives a dismissive sniff and looks down to the big Walker pistol, cocked and ready to fire.

The hammer falls, and the eruption from the loaded chamber of the horse pistol blasts through the lower neckline of the outlaw, soon followed by a splash of blood and the burning smell of black powder. The haze of gun-smoke hangs heavy as the gunshot man slumps at the side of the wagon. His eyes stare forward while his throat gurgles dark, oozing gore from his heaving torso.

The grizzled man holds the remainder of his ravaged neck and tries to speak through his severed windpipe. His eyes jump with panic and his head hangs to the side, nearly separated from his shoulders, pulsing with the outflow of lifeblood. He turns to the camp, takes a step and crumbles in a heap of gasping demise.

Exposed to the brutal raid, with the wagon cover removed, the family looks out to the surrounding scene. The pillaging of the murdered homesteading families is a gruesome spectacle. Some wagons still burn and a gust of wind swirls the dark smoke in a cyclone of debris that sweeps across the wreckage.

At the sound of the isolated gunshot, marauders, dressed in native buckskins and pilfered military garb, turn their attentions to the fallen bandit. The young boy braces the large Walker pistol between his knees and pulls back the heavy hammer again. He lifts it to the wagon's wooden sideboard and aims at a large man walking toward him. The imposing outlaw raises a hand carefully, as he halts his advance and calls out, "Don't you try 'n shoot me, boy!"

The boy briefly turns to his mother and sisters, who are gripped in fear, and then looks back to the advancing brigand. He squeezes the trigger and sends the fiery .44 lead-slug into the approaching man. Stumbling back, the bandit howls as the bullet tears through his side ribs and spins him to the ground.

"Kill that little scamp!"

The snap of pistols and rifles resumes for a short spell, and the boy watches as a gunshot smashes into his mother's head just below her eye. She slumps back, killed instantly, and the two teenage girls scream as they cling fearfully to the skirts of their dead protector. Slivers of the wood wagon jump and splinter into the air as a barrage of gunfire is directed at the wheeled vessel.

The boy ducks low and yanks back the hammer on the large pistol again. He peeks up as the shots cease momentarily and a horseback outlaw rides up alongside the wagon, with a rifle in hand. As the man turns broadside, the boy jumps up and discharges another chamber from the pistol that blasts into the horse-rider's leg. The bullet passes through the man's calf and saddle stirrup leather, into the belly of the mount. With a scream of pained agony, the horse rears and the rider tumbles to the ground.

The young defender tries to cock the large pistol again, as another marauder in partial native dress rushes from cover and takes hold of him. The fearsome looking man grabs the boy by the arm, jerks him from the wagon and slams him to the ground. In a thud, the boy hits hard and loses his grip on the pistol as he gasps for lost breath.

The long-haired man stands over him and pulls a large, glistening knife blade from its rawhide sheath as he speaks, "I'll teach you the way us Indians are accustomed to dealing with the whites…"

The knife wielding thug grabs a fistful of the boy's hair and lifts him from the ground. He puts the gleaming knife to the boy's scalp-line and the razor sharp edge of the blade slices into the thin skin over the skull. The numbing pain of the cut nearly paralyzes the boy as the blood starts to flow from the head wound. The boy blindly lashes out with his small fists and screams wildly.

The marauder laughs as he holds the child by the forelock and looks to the fresh blood on his blade. He readies to take the whole scalp when the young boy's fist smashes into the man's groin area, taking the wind from his bellows. The man gasps as he releases the cutting blade and tuft of held hair. He doubles over, howling in pain as he coughs to regain his breath.

The blood flowing freely down over his eyes from the scalp wound, the boy grabs up his Walker pistol and cocks it. He stabs it toward the attacker and fires point-blank into his chest. The man tumbles back with a smoking bullet hole in his middle, and the boy wipes the blood from his eyes with the back of his hand.

At the uncovered wagon, the two teenage girls are dragged from the clutches of their dead mother. The lead outlaw that caught the bullet across the ribs pulls the shrieking girls over the wagon-side to the ground and turns his dark gaze to the young boy with the Walker pistol standing nearby. He jabs a bloody finger in the air toward the boy and growls, "I'm gonna kill you next, boy!"

The boy cocks the large pistol again and fires from the hip. The explosion pushes the young shooter back to his heels and the whirling shot passes through the bottom lip of the man and exits his cheek. The outlaw turns his head momentarily and spits several fractured bloody teeth. He releases his grip on the girls and glares toward the young boy.

Time seems to stand static for a long moment as the youth looks from the angry outlaw to the carnage of friends and families scattered from the raid. Overwhelming fear envelopes the child and he turns to run away with the heavy weight of the Walker pistol clutched to his chest. Sounds of muted yelling and the vibrating pound of horses' hooves in pursuit wrack the boy with terror, as he dashes away from the horrible massacre.

The lower branches of trees rip at the running child's face while free-flowing blood from his scalp blurs his eyesight. Arriving at a steep cliff looming above a deep gorge, the young boy looks behind at his horseback pursuers weaving through the timber. The thunder and snort of the riders almost upon him, he pauses at the edge of the fateful abyss.

Through blood-tinged vision, the boy holds the pistol close and leaps out to the rocky, brush covered terrain dozens of feet below. The horseback marauders reach the edge of the cliff and stop their horses just shy of the steep drop-off. Rocks and debris crumble from the edge of the escarpment, and the riders pull back.

On the cliff above, the riders dance their horses around watching and waiting. Finally satisfied with the lack of any movement from below, they disappear from view and the landscape falls quiet again. A lone hawk soars in the sky, as smoke from the burning wagons drifts upward.

Chapter 2

A ranch cabin sits in the higher elevations of piney forests, opposite a butte and a cool mountain stream. The barn is set back in the trees from the dwelling and has several horses in the attached enclosure. A lone man walks from the sheltered lean-to alongside the corral and hitches his boot heel up on the four-rail fence to watch the grazing animals.

Dressed as a working rancher in high-topped leather boots, canvas pants and a drop-sleeved shirt, Holton Lang is a hard, lean man of the west. He was a U.S. Military scout in his varied past and still wears the well-worn cavalry hat from his years of service. Holton runs his hand along the smooth upper fence rail, worn down by horse rubbing, and looks around the stable. His gaze travels to the loyal mongrel dog that leaves its spot of shade to come over and sit near his leather-stacked boot heel. "Hey there, Dog ..."

Holton stares out to the evening horizon and faint signs of smoke draw his attention to the north. He gets a cold empty chill from remembrances of experienced violence as he studies the wafts of discolored sky. The repressed visions of long-ago battles pain him and he winces, trying to chase them from his troubled mind.

Dog watches his longtime human companion and turns to the distant sky, letting out a faint whimper. Holton glances down at the attentive dog and nods affirmative. "Yeah … we'll check it out." Another glimpse to the faraway smoke and the reflective rancher shakes off the feelings of bygone hurt and returns to the present.

Holton steps to the barn and grabs a well-worn pistol and holster belt from a peg near the doorway. With many years of familiarity, he buckles the supple leather billet and touches his hand over the worn walnut grip of the firearm. He slides the pistol from the holster and snaps open the loading gate to check the rounds in the cylinder, leaving the empty chamber under the hammer.

The faint burning memory from the smell of battle seems to heighten his senses. Holton looks out to the distant horizon with a quiet, steely gaze. He lets out a remorseful breath and sighs, "I hope it ain't what I think it is …"

~*~

In the high country of northern Arizona, a single horse and rider maneuver across rugged territory with nary a sign of civilized habitation. Following the lead of the raw-boned canine, the horseback figure with the aged cavalry hat studies the sky and proceeds at a determined pace. The unusually warm air hangs heavy and the quietness of the landscape seems to forebode an observation of mourning.

Holton sits astride his walking mount and looks around fleetingly as Dog sniffs his nose to the wind and trots the unseen trail ahead. Speaking aloud to the canine, he breaks the silence. "Should be there come sundown." He stares forward to the enduring trickles of smoke in the glowing afternoon sun and clenches his jaw. With a nudge of his spurred heels, he urges his horse up a rocky embankment and continues on toward the source of likely devastation.

~*~

The late day sun sets behind the mountains on toward evening, and Holton travels in the nearing dusk. He rides to a rough cut trail through the pines and shortly comes upon the ravaged wagon train assembly. The site of the massacre still smolders and burns with crippled wagons, putting a ghastly glow on the remaining earthly possessions strewn about.

Holton swallows the heavy lump in his throat and looks around at the looted bodies and the evident disregard for human life. He sits quiet and still, remaining on horseback in the twilight until Dog comes up and waits by his side. Holton blinks and stares down toward the dog, as the glow from the smoldering fires blaze a reflection in the man's eyes. He turns back to the wasteful carnage, and his eyes glisten with a wrenching pain from past memories.

After a time passes, the silhouetted form slowly walks his horse forward. Holton weaves his way through the destruction looking for any signs of life or survivors. He pauses over a pile of entangled forms gripping each other in a final moment of intimacy. A twitch of anger and remorse swells over him, and he tries to choke back strong emotions. The only sound in the coming night is the yip and howl from nearby coyotes waiting to ravage the spoils of devastation.

Chapter 3

The sun crests the horizon to the east and casts long broken shadows across the canyon carved landscape. Holton sits at the edge of the massacre site and looks despondently into the sullied disorder. The sun warms his shirt-back and he observes the eerie stillness quietly as Dog sits beside him, head lowered but watchful.

Carrion birds begin to circle overhead, and Holton rises to his feet. He walks to one of the half-burnt wagons, still smoldering, and grabs a shovel from alongside it. Holton looks around at the ghastly scene no longer concealed by darkness and moves to a tangled form, devoid of life. He stabs the shovel into the ground next to the ravaged corpse and begins the task of burying the hopes and dreams of the unfortunate souls traveling west.

~*~

Several mounds of rocks and sandy earth surround the site as Holton covers the dead where they lay. He looks to one of the few unburned wagons and winces at the sight of a woman slumped over the side with a gaping head wound. The look of eternal loss seems frozen on her sunken features as her stiff hands clasp for things since taken away.

Holton carefully lifts her from the supply-pillaged bed and lays her in the midday shade alongside the wagon. The sweat beads up and forms lines down from his temples as Holton stands looking at the young woman, thinking on her lost potential for a life in the frontier. He looks to another leather-clad, long-haired male corpse near the wagon and instantly senses he was not from the pioneer group, but a casualty of the unrelenting raiders.

The man in dirty buckskins, with empty ammunition bandoliers across his chest, still clasps the neck wound where he finally bled out. A surrounding puddle of darkened ground appears black with lifeblood, soaked and dried into the rocky earthen surface. Holton studies the area around the wagon and spots several other splashes of blood along with unshod horse and booted foot traffic.

Holton breaks the stillness with a low whistle, and Dog scampers from the brush. The canine stands beside Holton obediently as they look over the destruction. He glimpses the animal picking through the various scents and whispers low, "They put up a good fight …"

Pacing the area and reading the jumbled markings on the ground, he follows the prior actions between the dead bodies. He momentarily gazes up to the surrounding site with its many mounds of casualties and turns back to the tracks leading out of camp. Dropping to a knee, Holton closely studies a set of smaller boot tracks and the impressions of a horse print directly over-laying. He turns back to the wagon with the dead woman below and grimaces.

The midday sun sits high overhead. Dog keeps a watchful eye on Holton, as he traces the path of the smaller footed figure followed by horseback pursuers. They pass through the trees, occasionally losing the trail on rock but shortly picking up the signs further on. They come to the last traces of prints at the brink of a tall ridge.

Holton takes a knee again, blinks away faint hopes of salvation and seems conflicted, as he reads the finality of the chase in the obvious imprints of broken rock and mud. "Somebody took a helluva leap from here." He looks over as Dog leans out and sniffs the air below. He peers down at the steep drop-off and winces at the improbable outcome from such a jump. "We'll finish the job at hand first then take a look below."

The two walk the distance back to the wagon site, and Holton pauses as they near the perimeter. The hairs rise on his neck and he looks around inquisitively at the quiet terrain. Several shadowy birds spread their wings and circle overhead, but the coyotes and all else have quieted.

The static air seems silent and uncommonly still. Holton steps around one of the wagons, followed by Dog. The alert canine hunkers low and begins to growl.

"What is it Dog?"

Holton stands near the shot woman laid at the wagon. He hesitates while listening into the wooded surroundings and reaches for the shovel. The sound of a heavy pistol click breaks the quietness, and Dog lets out a rumbling snarl. Holton turns to face a young boy with his features masked with dried blood and a large Walker horse pistol in hand, pointed directly toward him.

"Easy there, boy … what's yer name?"

The boy's jaw begins to quiver, and he lets out a faint whisper. "My name is Jules Ward …" The two stare at each other a moment until the boy takes a step nearer and raises the Walker pistol's aim higher. "Step away from my mother."

Dog growls louder and Holton puts his hand out to quiet him. He holds the shovel in one hand and waits calmly, as the boy steps closer.

"Hello Jules. Put down that big iron, and we can talk." Holton observes the look of a half-crazed child showing through the boy's blood-crusted features.

The long barrel of the pistol wavers, and Jules mutters loudly, "You're one of them … I'll kill you!" Jules' eyes flash with hatred, and he starts to squeeze the trigger. Quickly, Holton swings out with the shovel and knocks the pistol's aim away as it discharges into the rocky ground. The boy tries to pull back the hammer again, as he cries out in shocked anguish, "I'll kill you!"

Holton rushes forward and grabs hold of the boy in a restraining hug. Jules wiggles and thrashes for a good while then finally collapses in a fit of weeping tears. Holton holds the sobbing boy tight and pulls his sniffling head into his shoulder. "It's okay kid, I got ya."

Dog remains alert and wary, as Holton holds the crying child in a tight embrace. The grown man sinks to his knees and embraces the trauma stricken boy. Jules eases into convulsive whimpers, and Holton glances over as Dog curls up on the ground next to the dead woman.

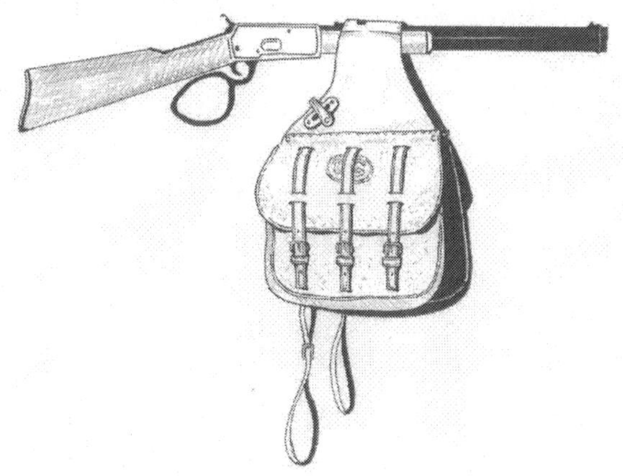

Chapter 4

Holton rides along, with Dog following close beside the horse. Behind the cantle of his saddle, the young boy sits on the rump of Holton's mount with his legs dangling over the saddle pouches. The weather is cool and fair, as they travel across the rugged terrain southwest toward Holton's ranch and cabin.

The stoic form of the western figure rides straight in the saddle, without looking back at the quiet boy. Jules is mostly cleaned-up, with a bandage around his forehead, but he still has a bit of the far-away crazed look in his eyes. He sits loosely on the horse's hindquarter, with the big Walker pistol laid across his lap. Holton listens all around but keeps his attention forward, while Jules notices Dog put his nose to the breeze and slip off silently into the surrounding brush.

The tandem riders slow their pace, and Holton glances back at the boy as they ease down a rocky grade. He starts to speak, then thinks better of it and remains quiet. They continue to ride along silently until they finally come up to the front entrance of the ranch.

Holton looks up to the aged, wooden sign hanging below the high crossed beam. He clenches his jaw as he silently stares at the *Nichols "5" Ranch* heading, then gives a casual salute.

Jules whispers almost inaudibly, "You Nichols?"

"Nope. Belonged to a man I respected."

"He dead?"

Speaking over his shoulder to the young boy, Holton gestures to the carved marker on the yonder hilltop. "He's passed on. Neither of us had any sort of kin to speak of, 'cept each other." The mention of family quiets the boy, and they ride in silence down the lane. Dog pops from the brush and joins them, as they continue the path toward the cabin and outbuildings.

~*~

The day has faded away toward evening, and the sun begins to dip behind the distant hills. Holton steps out from the barn and looks toward the cabin. On the shaded porch sits the young boy, with the big horse pistol in his lap, staring out to the horizon.

Holton looks down to the pistol hung at his side and the big lever loop rifle in hand. He angles his jaw and spits to the side. "Men and their guns ..." He glances over to the bucket of tools by the corral and ponders the implements of survival on the frontier. The words of men wiser than himself echo in his memories, as he reflects on the use of a gun and the respect for its power.

Holton walks up to the cabin followed by Dog and stops at the bottom step to the porch. He looks at Jules who continues his silent, faraway gaze. "How you doin', boy?" The boy's eyes dart to Holton a short second before looking back to the horizon. Holton notices the boy's lip quiver as the youth tries to control his raw emotions, and he speaks to him again.

"You hungry?"

With a slight nod Jules blinks and swallows silently.

"Good 'nuff." Holton climbs the wooden slab steps, passes by Jules and notices the boy clench the Walker pistol tighter. He pauses at the cabin door and looks down at the troubled child. Not finding any significant words of comfort, Holton sets his rifle near the doorway and moves to the inside.

~*~

The interior of the ranch cabin contains years of clutter from the former owner, Charlie Nichols. Upon receiving the ranch setup from his departed friend, Holton never had the inclination to move things or make them his own. His sleeping arrangement is still made on a pallet of animal hides and blankets by the stone fireplace, while across the room Charlie's vacant bunk goes unused.

Holton sits across from Jules at the wood-planked table in the middle of the room as they both quietly eat venison stew from carved bowls. Pleased, the seasoned westerner watches the young boy eat hungrily and grins. "Ain't lost yer appetite I see?"

Jules glances up at him and continues chewing silently. The smile fades from the grownup man's features and he nods. "I ain't much for talk either."

Holton finishes his bowl of food and wipes the back of his hand across his mouth. He sits back, scratches the whisker stubble on his cheek, and looks to the stone fireplace. The lingering smell of stew comes from the iron pot hanging on a swing arm that is pulled away from the cook fire.

Holton looks to the dog curled up on the floor, contented and enjoying the evening warmth of the nearby coals. "Yer welcome to live her awhile. It ain't much ..."

Without looking up, Jules stops his eating and his shoulders heave upward as he starts to breathe heavily. Between panting breaths, strong words come from the young boy. "I'll kill 'em ..."

Holton turns from his fire gazing and looks at the child across the table. He's not sure what to make of the odd reaction to his hospitality. "What?"

Jules stares up at Holton, with a murderous look of rage. "I'll kill them all."

A little off-put, Holton studies the distraught look on the young boy's features. He glances to the bled-through bandage covering the boy's forehead and returns his gaze to those troubled young eyes. "Won't change anything."

"They'll be dead."

Holton sits and thinks a moment. "I'll take you to Prescott 'n talk to the County Sheriff."

Jules firmly sets down his eating utensil and stares hard at Holton. "No, you won't."

"How's that?"

"They killed both my Mama 'nd Paw, took my sisters… I have to kill 'em myself."

Holton studies the boy's determined intent consuming his youthful features. "They took hostages?" Jules nods quietly and Holton continues, "Who were these men?"

"They were Indians or Mexicans and some were dressed like soldiers, partly." The boy's face starts to contort with painful memories, and his hand goes to the grip of the Walker pistol nested in his lap.

Holton pushes his bowl of food aside, leaning forward on the rough-hewn table. "Damn …" He thinks on the boy with barely a decade of years on him. "Did you see them all?"

"I shot some of 'em."

As the two sit across the table from each other, Holton watches Jules pick up his utensil with his free hand and push the last of his food around in the bowl.

"How many were there?"

"A dozen that I would recognize."

Holton studies the boy a while and chooses his words carefully for the delicate situation. "How do you expect to find 'em and do all this killin'?"

The boy shoves his meal dish aside, pulls the heavy Walker pistol from his lap and slams it on the wood-slab table. "I've killed some already. I will again, until I find my sisters."

Holton folds his hands on the table and stares ahead at Jules. "I'm telling you this, not 'cause it's the easiest to do, but because it's the best thing for you ..." Holton, a comparably older, experienced man and a veteran of fighting wars with and against both the Indians and U.S. Military, takes a deep calming breath. Holton's heart aches as he looks into the familiar anguish of the young boy's eyes and continues, "You got to let it go. They didn't take many captives as far as I could tell. You're sisters are most likely dead or worse, and nothing you do can bring them back."

Jules stares at the large pistol on the table before him. "There's nothing anyone can do to stop me."

Holton looks down at his own clasped hands and peers up at the aggrieved boy's expression. "All right. I can take you to Camp Verde, where they have a military post. They might have some knowledge of these marauders."

"What will they do?"

"If these men who took your sisters are selling goods or trading them to the Mexicans or Indians, the military might know where they are headed to do it."

Jules smooths his small fingers over the oversized Walker handgun. He looks up at Holton and shakes his head. "Many thanks for what you did for the others, mister, but I don't need your help."

Holton opens his palms and looks to the dirt stains and shovel calluses from recent digging. He rubs a thumb along the rough pad below his fingers and looks up gravely at the young boy. "If you're lookin' to survive this thing, you'll need all the help you can get."

Chapter 5

The chill of morning is still in the air, as the sun crests the mountains to the east and shines brightly across the valley. Holton steps outside the cabin to the porch and glances at the roll of blankets where the young boy slept. All traces of Jules are gone, including the large Walker pistol.

Holton looks over the area and scratches his chest through his exposed undershirt. Rubbing his foot on the porch post, he adjusts the soft leather heel of the Indian-style moccasin on his feet. The nearby horses nicker for morning feed, and Holton looks down to Dog sitting at the top of the steps watching the corral.

"That young'un is up early." Dog lets out an answering bark and dashes down the steps toward the corral where, instead of four horses, there are only three. Holton stares a moment in disbelief then looks down the lane toward the distant ranch gate. He looks again to the corral and murmurs, "Damn..."

Half-dressed, Holton reaches inside the cabin doorway, grabs his rifle and jumps down the steps toward the barn. He quickly searches the interior of the outbuilding and surveys the remaining horses in the corral. Dog comes over, and sits where Holton's saddle and blanket hang over a log stand under the lean-to.

The faraway horizon is clear of any sign of a rider. Holton studies the surrounding hills and quietly shakes his head. He looks to Dog, who averts his gaze, lowering his nose.

"That kid is sure something; he took my best horse."

~*~

Outfitted in a buckskin frontier shirt with a fringed bib, Holton places a set of saddlebags on the log-slab table in the cabin. He wraps items of food with cloth and tucks them inside the leather-flapped compartments. The former military scout looks to his rifle propped against a ladder-back chair. He pulls two boxes of cartridges from the cupboard shelf and stuffs them in the pouch.

Holton secures the straps on his saddlebags and heaves the load over his shoulder. He grabs up a rolled blanket along with his rifle and gives the room a fleeting glance. His eyes scan for other possibles needed on the intended journey.

"C'mon Dog, let's go."

Stopping at the doorway, Holton turns and looks back into the small cabin. He takes it all in: the cold stone fireplace, the accumulated clutter of another man's belongings and the empty bunk of Charlie Nichols. He silently accepts the possibility of this being the last farewell and pulls the creaking door shut behind him.

Followed closely by the independent-minded canine, Holton rides north toward the wagon massacre. He scans the ground for fresh tracks and glances back at Dog sniffing for unfamiliar scents in the warm breeze. They shadow the recognized trail from days prior, but Holton appears troubled.

Come midday, Holton steers his mount to the location of the recent homesteader massacre. The site is undisturbed, and the burnt wagons are grim reminders of the many deceased, laid beneath earthen mounds. Holton turns in the saddle and observes as Dog sits at the edge of the burial grounds, watching keenly. He urges his horse forward and slowly rides farther into the graveyard.

Holton looks to his borrowed horse tied at a broken wagon and calls, "Boy … C'mon out."

Jules steps from around his family's abandoned wagon and stands before Holton with his large Walker pistol in hand. "You gonna try 'n lynch me?

Confused, Holton looks down at the troubled child. "Lynch ya?"

"You come for the horse I stole, didn't you?"

The hardened Westerner relaxes in the saddle and stares down at the boy. He sees the abundance of anxiety and fear deliberately concealed by the ignorance of youth. "I come for you."

"I ain't going back."

Holton steps down from his horse and looks around the primitive burial markers. He observes the boy standing over his mother's grave and sighs with a heavy heart. "Nope, didn't figure you would."

~*~

The darkness of night has shrouded the grim reminders of death buried in the ground. Holton and Jules sit near a small campfire and eat a cooked jackrabbit. The ghostly shadows of broken wagons in the background flicker at the edge of the firelight. The young boy's eyes glow in the low light, as he peers up to the buckskin clad figure seated across from him.

"You can track them?"

Holton turns his attention to Jules as he chews and nods quietly. The young boy analyzes Holton's leather fringe shirt. He notices dark patches of aged-dry blood and scars from battles long ago.

"Are you part Indian?"

"My mother was Apache."

The boy sits with the Walker pistol tight in his lap. He fingers the gun nervously in the firelight. "The Apache raid and kill people."

"So do soldiers 'n other folks."

Jules lowers his eyes to the flickering flames of the small campfire. "Those men who took my sisters ... some were Indians."

Holton finishes chewing and studies the boy sitting across from him. He recognizes the youth's loss of innocence and tries to impart compassion.

"There are good people and bad people. Doesn't matter the shade of yer skin or the uniform ya wear. I was raised with the military when both my parents were gone. Later I lived with the Apache and took a wife ... Both I called home, and there were faults with each."

The boy narrows his gaze at Holton inquisitively. "I didn't see no hint of a woman at your spread."

"Nope."

A long silence ensues, as Holton turns a glistening eye to the lively licks of firelight. Jules stares at the seasoned cavalry hat pushed back on Holton's forehead and asks, "Have you hunted men before?"

"I've done things to survive... things I felt right in doing and things I'm not proud of."

They both sit quietly in the light of the dancing flames. Dog lounges in the area between them with his head down, dark eyes passing between the two.

Jules' shoulders begin to quiver, and tears roll down his cheeks. The boy tries to hold back his emotions, but they are overwhelming. Not knowing how to react, Holton averts his eyes and turns to the darkness as the boy speaks. "I let them get taken ... I could have saved them."

Holton lets his gaze return and shakes his head slightly. "I doubt it."

Through puffing sobs, Jules wipes the streaming tears from his face. "I shot three of them, and when another came at me, I left my sisters and run off."

Holton gestures to the recent graveyard behind them. "You'd be dead like them others if you hadn't."

"With Paw gone, it was my job to protect the family. Mama was kilt, and I abandoned my sisters to save myself."

Holton nods with sentiments of solace glistening in his eyes. He looks at the pre-teen boy and sees the makings of a man. "Surviving often has nothing to do with bravery."

Jules pulls a blanket up around his shoulders and lies over on his side next to the fire. His body trembles with sobs as he buries his tear-streaked face in the coarse, woolen wrap. Holton remains silent and watches the boy weep. He wrestles with the unfamiliar urge to comfort another being and sits quietly while the campfire slowly fades to embers.

Chapter 6

Riding two abreast, Holton and Jules travel on horseback following the trail of the raiders. They head southeast as the sun rises over the horizon before them. The tracks are easily discernible, with fresh wagon ruts following the larger grouping of shod and unshod horse prints.

Jules rides nearer to Holton and stares down at the dog faithfully trotting alongside. "What's the dog's name?"

"Dog."

"Ya don't call him anything else?"

"Jest, Dog."

The boy rides quiet with his thoughts. Then he looks Holton over curiously, eyeing the fringe hanging on his buckskin shirt. "Don't Apache eat dogs?"

"Hungry people will eat jest 'bout most things." Holton looks at Jules wryly and grins. "You don't name things you might have to eat."

For the first time since their meeting, Jules seems to relax, and a hint of a smile crosses his features. He pauses a moment, and stares down at Dog, then back up at Holton. "You wouldn't …"

Holton shrugs and continues on. He raises a fringe-lined arm and gestures toward the trail ahead. "This path they're travelin' on will lead us straight into Camp Verde. If they're not still around and the military don't have some answers for us, we're gonna have a hard time picking up a trail once it mixes with other comin's 'n goin's."

Jules looks around to the many surrounding ridges and valleys in the landscape. "Are you sure this is the right trail?"

Holton nods grimly. "With the job they left behind, there warn't no need to take caution in cover'n their tracks."

~*~

On the road outside the military post at Camp Verde, Holton and Jules pass through a tumble-down village of dark-skinned Indians. As they ride through the neglected home sites, the young boy looks at the obvious poverty and half-naked children running around. "What kind of fort is this?"

"Ain't a fort so much as a place for the gov'ment to keep an eye on the local population."

"Why? The people all look mostly starved and tired."

Holton continues riding past the village toward the grouping of wood-framed structures of the military base. "Gov'ment policy is to keep "em hungry and beat-down. Figures it keeps 'em from hostilities."

Jules turns in the saddle seat and looks back at several Indian youngsters who, have stopped playing and are starring back at him. "Seems to work."

"Nope, jest makes 'em angry and resentful."

The two mounted riders steer their horses to one of the main military buildings near the parade grounds. Holton stops his mount before the hitching rail and turns a serious gaze toward Jules. "I'm gonna need you to sit tight and wait here with Dog and the horses. I will talk with the commanding officer."

"I want to go in and hear what they have to say."

Holton looks around to affirm that no one is near enough to listen to what he has to say. "The thing is ... if they find you've been orphaned, they're gonna take you into custody here at the fort till they can place you with family somewheres."

"My family is all dead 'cept my sisters."

"Then they will raise you in a special home."

"Like they do with the Indians?"

"Something like that."

The tall buckskin-clad figure steps down and peers over his saddle at Jules. He studies the boy a moment and senses the youth's unwavering drive and determination. "Don't talk to anyone and tuck that hog-leg away so's you don't attract extra attention."

Jules looks down at the long-barreled pistol across his lap. He passes his thumb over one of the percussion capped chambers on the cylinder, clenches his jaw and stares back at Holton. "You best not try to pull any tricks on me. I'm gonna hunt them men down with your help or not."

Holton acknowledges the kid with a nod, possessing a deep understanding of the boy's thirst for his sisters' recovery and revenge for his family. He glances over at the nearby canine and tilts his head toward Jules. "Dog, stay with 'im."

The dog stares silently as the young boy pivots in the saddle seat and tucks the Walker pistol between the high cantle and rolled blanket. He sits the horse quiet and watches Holton enter the military building headquarters.

~*~

As time passes, Jules climbs down from his mount to stretch his legs. He looks to the dog sitting in the shade from the shadow of his horse and joins him. They sit and calmly observe together as troopers march across the parade grounds and several riders pass by.

A commotion from the grouping of tent saloons and mercantile sutler setups attracts their attention. Jules watches as a Mexican man is forcibly shoved from one of the large canvas structures into the dirt path of the street. There is a brief exchange of words, and he stumbles, visibly drunk, and mounts a horse standing untethered near several others.

The Mexican reaches over the animal's neck for the dropped reins, turning the steed several times before he finally has them gathered in hand. Sitting upright in the saddle, the man pulls on his wide, sombrero hat which hangs by a leather string around his neck. After a while, he gets his bearings and rides toward Jules and Dog.

The lounging pair on the ground watches the heavily intoxicated rider and a flash of terror swells over the young boy as the recognized Mexican outlaw passes by. Jules instinctively grabs for his gun. Realizing it is not in his lap, he looks up to the walnut grips of the large pistol tucked behind his saddle seat. He watches the backside of the dirty bandit, as the drunken man rides the trail east, away from the camp.

Chapter 7

A soldier steps up to the administrations structure of Camp Verde and marches across the front walkway. The heavy plank door of the building opens and Holton steps out on the wooden porch. He stops in the shadow of the overhanging roof and winces into the midday brightness. Holton looks to where he left the boy with the dog and seems mildly irritated at the sight of his own saddled horse, standing alone.

"Damn kid ..."

Holton hops down the steps, drops to a knee and studies the faint tracks near his horse. He squats on his heels, lays the big-loop rifle across his lap and looks to the east. After a moment of quiet deliberation, Holton moves around his animal, swings into the saddle seat and kicks his horse into an easy lope. With neither Dog nor the boy in sight, Holton follows the trail from the camp toward the rising hills beyond.

~*~

Hours pass on the trail as Jules travels horseback along the Mogollon Ridge. The young boy rides with a floppy hat pulled low over his bandaged head. He watches the path before him and the single tracks of a horse leading away. Not far behind, nearly out of sight, Dog slinks along after the boy. The lean animal keeps low to the shade along the scrubby brush skirting the trail.

The traveled pathway narrows to a bluff high to one side and a cluster of rocks crowding in on the other. Jules holds up his mount and notices the tracks he was following in the corridor have been deliberately scratched out. He studies them a moment before his horse balks and shies away. The boy checks the horse's retreat and catches a glimpse of a man's shadow on the rocks just as a voice calls out.

"Eay! Hold it there, boy!" The half-drunk Mexican man steps out from behind the pile of boulders and raises a Sharps carbine at Jules. His voice slurs as he lines up the rifle sights on the young boy. "Why do you follow me, hijo?"

Jules grips the Walker pistol in his small hand and tries to pull back the hammer while holding a fistful of reins in his other. The Mexican's eyes lower to the oversized pistol, and he smiles drunkenly. In a flash of movement, with the rifle still raised, the man pulls off his sugarloaf sombrero and waves it belligerently in the face of the horse. The startled animal skitters back a few steps and rears up in defense.

Jules tumbles out of the saddle, losing his grip on the handle of his pistol, and crashes to the rocky ground with an awkward thud. Before the boy can regain his lost breath or find the dropped pistol, the Mexican man is standing over top of him, staring down.

"So, you want to hurt me, un pequeño?"

The young boy heaves for air in his chest, and his eyes dart around for the fallen pistol. The side of a dusty boot heel pushes the boy back. The Mexican reaches down and pulls off Jules' hat, revealing the head bandage. The noticeably inebriated man leans closer, with the smell of mescal ripe on his breath. "Do I know you?"

In the shadow of the larger man, Jules looks up slowly and eyes the fancy handled knife on the Mexican's belt. The boy's eyes travel further up to connect with the questioning stare from the confused figure above. Jules regains his nerve and utters, "I'm goin' to kill you."

With a toothy smile, the Mexican grabs Jules by the shirt collar and jerks him to his feet. "That is not a nice thing for a sweet boy like you to be saying to me."

The hot fermented breath of the man burns the boy's eyes, and the fierce look of vengeful determination returns to the youth's features. The Mexican holds Jules up by a handful of shirt and looks at him, perplexed. "Why you follow me?"

Jules quickly reaches out and grabs at the fancy knife handle. He tears it from the leather belt sheath and stabs it into the stomach of the Mexican man. Stunned, the man pushes Jules back to the ground and looks down. He stares with disbelief at his own knife buried hilt-deep in his belly. Due to shock, the sensation of pain hasn't set in yet and the Mexican man stands looking down at Jules incredulously.

"Mi Madre de Dios … you stuck me good!"

Still holding the Sharps rifle, the man braces himself in his stance and pulls the stuck knife out in a quick jerk of motion. He stares down at the shimmering object as blood drips from the blade and, as if only his feelings were damaged, the Mexican turns his troubled gaze toward the boy on the ground before him. "Why you do that?"

Jules begins to tremble and the words come out shakily. "You killed my family and took my sisters!"

The Mexican reflects quietly a moment then gives a huff. "Huh, I tell them … the boy must have wings to fly off a cliff like that."

The man gently lays down the rifle on the dirt path and advances on the boy. He winces as he holds his injured abdomen and points the bloody knife at Jules. "We may not be able to sell you with the others when I finish carving on you."

Jules scoots away on his bottom as the Mexican approaches. As he leans forward to slice at the boy, Dog leaps from the brush with snarling teeth and a snap of canine jaws. The Mexican screams like a small child as the dog grips his shoulder and thrashes with the full weight of his four-legged body.

As the man and dog wrestle on the ground, Jules quickly jumps to his feet and grabs the discarded Sharps carbine. He pulls back the rifle hammer and calls out to the aggressive canine. "Dog, get back!"

With a fierce growl, the attacking animal releases his grip and backs up a few steps. The Mexican man holds his wounds and crawls away to the rocks. He leans back on the cool, shaded stone surface, looking down to his bleeding belly and teeth-torn shoulder. "Why you do this to me? I don't have your sisters …"

Jules steps forward with the rifle cocked and ready. "Where are they?"

"They take them to Fort Tularosa. Maybe sell them there or move on … wherever they get the best price."

The young boy raises the short rifle and aims the thick barrel at the man's face. "You will take me to them?"

Amused, the Mexican looks to his sliced gut and ravaged arm. "No, you hurt me bad … I will jest try to kill you. You best shoot me now, or we will both die."

"Are my sisters alive?"

"Sí … but they will not give them to you."

Jules stares hard and a tear drips down his dusty cheek. "I will kill them all."

The Mexican smiles faintly and coughs, then eyes the dog staring at him hungrily.

"Maybe you will … do you feed that dog?"

"No. He's not mine."

His eyes still watching the growling beast, the injured man shakes his head mournfully. "When I am dead, and if you are not, could you have him not eat me? I am a good Catholic, and it is not proper to be eaten by an ugly dog."

Dog lets out a low rumbling snarl and licks the saliva from his teeth. The young boy lowers the rifle's aim and looks over at the protective canine. "He does as he chooses."

The Mexican man whimpers slightly as he shifts himself on the rocky face, and the shock of his injuries begins to make him sweat. "You are not a nice boy. I think I should kill you!"

"You will take me to my sisters." When Jules looks away to his isolated surroundings, the Mexican man sees an opportunity and lunges forward. In the split second of the man's attack, a resounding blast from the rifle suddenly echoes in the rocks. A cloud of black-powder smoke clears, and the young boy stands his ground with his finger pulled back on the trigger.

Rifle-shot to the head, the Mexican falls limp at Jules' feet and twitches several involuntary death spasms. The young boy drops the rifle, astonished, and slowly steps away to gather up the reins of his horse. He looks around for his Walker pistol and spots it at the base of a scraggly bush.

With a wary eye ever-glancing to the dead figure sprawled nearby, Jules lifts his revolver from the ground, uncocks it and blows the sandy grit from the cylinder. He tucks the long barrel in the space behind the slick-fork saddle horn and climbs the stirrups to gain his seat. At the edge of the trail, Dog watches the boy, and Jules looks down at the protecting mongrel dog.

"Thanks Dog." Jules looks east, turns his horse and trots off down the trail.

~*~

On a piling of rocks, a rifle-shot distance away, Holton observes over the lined-up sights of his big-loop lever gun. He watches Jules disappear on the trail behind the bluff, as his furry companion, Dog, sits patiently watching the dead marauder. Holton uncocks his rifle, stands and climbs to a taller rock platform.

The alert dog turns his attention to the silhouetted western figure and watches patiently toward Holton. The buckskin clad observer holds his rifle across his chest and gives an affirming nod. Without hesitation, Dog dashes away along the trail after the young boy.

Chapter 8

The late afternoon sun dips golden in the western sky as Holton climbs down from the overlooking rock formation. With rifle in hand, he steps from a low plateau onto his waiting horse's back and rides slowly along the trail toward the dead Mexican. The warm, high-desert air is quiet and still, with only the soft clopping sound from the feet of the sure-footed mount.

Holton arrives at the scene of recent struggle between man and boy and looks down at the lifeless body as it bleeds out into the dry sandy ground. Stepping from his saddle rig, he glances around the area and kneels beside the shot, stabbed and canine-mauled Mexican. Holton eyes the ivory-handled pistol at the dead man's side and nudges the body over to unbuckle the holster belt. He pulls the leather-looped cartridge rig from the body and wraps it with a swing around the holstered revolver.

Holton tucks the bundled gun and holster set under his arm and picks up the Sharps rifle from the ground. He stands and thinks over the situation a moment before leading his horse around the rocks to where the Mexican man's horse stands tied to a tree. With his mount close behind, he approaches the tethered animal and tucks the pistol rig in a cloth canvas war bag slung over the rawhide pommel.

Holton looks the fancy riding rig over and peers back around his horse at the sprawled feet of the dead man. He lifts the canvas bag from the decorated saddle and loops the tie drawstring over his own saddle horn. After he tucks the Sharps rifle behind the cantle of his waiting mount, he returns to the ownerless horse and begins to loosen the cinch strap.

The rawhide and leather-trimmed Mex saddle drops to the ground with a creaking thud. Holton eases the bridle over the horse's forelock and lets the bit fall from its mouth. He smooths his hand over the back of the unburdened animal and gives the steed's rump a solid tap. The horse turns alerted ears forward and trots away, free to range for itself.

The distinct trail to the east lies before him, and Holton looks to the faraway dust haze rising from the young boy's travel. He stands and watches awhile before mounting up. With thoughts of the young man's hard determination and a reassured feeling that Dog follows after, Holton urges his horse onward at an easy pace.

~*~

The dusky light of evening shadows the landscape as Jules sits near his horse at the edge of the trail. A blanket wrapped around his shoulders, he shivers from the coming chill of the desert night. Dog sits nearby and raises his head, listening into the nearing darkness. The quiet clop of horse hooves comes down the trail, and Jules takes out his Walker pistol to position across his lap.

The horseback rider draws nearer and pauses when the loud and distinct click of the large pistol hammer is heard pulling back. A familiar voice calls out peaceably from the approaching nightfall.

"Don't shoot, boy."

Jules stands and tries to peer into the faint light. "Mister Lang?"

"Who were you expecting?"

The boy pauses a moment to think then lowers the pistol. "Come on then."

Holton rides up with his features shadowed by the darkening night sky. He stares down at the young boy awhile then turns his studied gaze to the horse secured to a low bush by the bridle reins. "You shouldn't leave that horse tied like that at the mouth. It would be better if you hobbled him."

Jules looks up at Holton silently and nods. The horseback man looks over to the dog, who sits obediently waiting and watching. He turns back to the boy and notices the blanket over his small, shivering shoulders. "You know how to make a fire?"

"If I did, I'd have one now."

Holton steps down from his horse and begins to unsaddle. "Gather some wood and I'll show you."

~*~

Set back from the trail a safe distance, Holton and Jules sit near a small campfire with the unsaddled horses hobbled nearby. Holton offers the boy a piece of dried deer meat, and Jules takes it hungrily. He looks the boy over and watches him awhile before speaking.

"What's yer plan now?"

Jules chews a mouthful of the jerky and glances up. "I'm going to find my sisters." Holton lets out a low grunt, under his breath. "Well, that's a sight better than your kill 'em all plan." The boy stares at Holton across the small fire, confused as to whether or not he is joking. "I will kill them."

Holton nods and considers his next words a moment. "If you would have waited at the camp, I learned that those marauders hail from east of here."

"I found that out myself."

Holton watches the young boy and notices his seemingly hard determination is now tainted with remorse. "Did you aim to kill that man back there on the trail?"

The boy lowers his head ashamed and stares at the small fire. "He forced me to it."

"Was he one of the gang who raided your family?"

Jules sits quietly then nods slightly.

Holton speaks in a slightly hushed, sympathetic tone. "He would have killed you given the chance, so there is nothing more to think about."

The two sit staring at the orange flames that jump and curl around the remaining tinder. Holton looks out to the dark landscape and the star-filled sky. He notices

Jules watching him and makes eye contact in the shadowy darkness.

The boy speaks in a low whisper as if to keep the information from the unseen mysteries of the coming night. "The man back there said they might try to sell my sisters near Fort Tularosa."

"Possible ... They will probably unload a lot of their loot there, but I hear the slave trading is with Mexican-Apache further south or the Comanchero bands in Texas." Holton watches the juvenile orphaned boy staring at him for guidance. "I want to help you but I can't be of service if you go riding off without me. Do you understand?"

Jules nods and pulls the wool blanket up on his shoulders. "If you help me find my sisters and don't keep me from killing them who took 'em, I'll stick along with you, Mister Lang."

The experienced westerner sniffs and nods agreeable. "Most jest call me Holton."

"Yes, sir."

Jules adjusts the blanket snug around himself, and his face cracks weepily from the confusion of pent up emotions just below the surface. The sympathetic man watches as the young boy lays back and tries to sleep through broken, quiet sobs of grieving. Starring out to the dark surroundings, Holton sits quiet and listens to the empty night, as the firelight flickers out to a soft red glow of embers.

Chapter 9

The established trail toward Nuevo Mexico follows along the lower reaches of the Mogollon Ridge. Holton and Jules ride alongside each other in the cool, early part of the day. The older man looks over at the boy who sits comfortable in the saddle, with his legs dangling on each side of the tall horse.

Jules still stubbornly clings to the Walker pistol in his lap, as he holds the reins easy in his left hand. Holton adjusts his hat, glances over at the pre-war cap-and-ball percussion revolver, then grunts, "What are we gonna do about that oversized horse pistol you're intent on carrying?" The boy looks down at his grip on the firearm and then over at Holton, with a stern countenance. "I intend to make use of it."

"If you can't pull that hammer back with one hand, you're more apt to drop it than shoot it."

"I've put some of 'em down with it already."

Holton nods and eases his horse closer. He takes hold of Jules' horse's headstall and halts both their mounts. "Let me see you use it." He gestures toward a broken off tree stump, "Slap a load of lead into that, boy."

With effort, Jules raises the heavy pistol and pulls back the hammer with his left palm. He pulls the trigger, hitting his mark, and the horse under him hops sideways in reaction to the explosive discharge. Clinging on the saddle, Jules drops the Walker pistol to the ground and settles his mount. The boy steals a quick obstinate glance to Holton and climbs down to retrieve his gun.

Holton opens the cloth war-bag on his pommel and pulls out the dead Mexican's fancy-handled Colt and holster. "This holster-belt rig is too big for ya but the shooter is more yer size." He tosses the wrapped gun and holster rig down to Jules who catches it awkwardly. The two stare at each other until Holton gives a nod.

"Go ahead, try it on."

Jules looks down at his Walker pistol, defiantly reaches up to his full height and tucks it in the half-seat of the empty saddle. Holton eases his horse around the other animal and watches, amused, as the young boy unwinds the gun-belt and holster. Jules puts the cartridge belt to his narrow waist and loops it around himself nearly twice.

Shy with embarrassment, Jules looks up at Holton and hitches the oversized cartridge belt over his shoulder. He draws the Mexican's fancy shooter from the holster and looks over the elaborately engraved gun barrel. Jules aims at the tree again and pulls back easy on the smooth, tuned-action. The snap of the barking pistol seems to fit better in his small hand as he fires a shot followed by another, all hitting at their mark.

Holton holds the anxious horses from skittering away and nods, impressed. "Alright kid, I see you can shoot." He takes out the remaining contents of the cloth sack and tosses the empty bag to Jules. "Tuck that thing away and don't get it out unless you need it to survive."

"Yes sir." The boy opens the side loading gate and ejects the spent cartridges. He reloads the empty chambers from the ammo belt, wraps the holstered gun in a bundle and tucks it in the sack. Holton watches Jules climb the stirrups into the saddle, hang the war-bag on the horn and adjust in the saddle to hold the Walker pistol in his lap again.

The patient chaperone sits astride his mount and looks to the young boy, strangely. "Yer still gonna hold onto that hog-leg?"

"Yep."

Holton looks back at Dog who stares up at him blankly then returns his gaze to the boy. "Suit yerself."

~*~

At the perimeter of Fort Tularosa, Holton and Jules approach the few wood-framed buildings and a scattering of log cabins and tents. Several wagons are parked near the corrals which are full of stock being trained for military service. Lines of trooper tents are set up for the soldiers along the south border of the camp.

Holton glances over at Jules as he rides alongside and whispers low, "You follow my lead, stay close and keep that smoke-wagon out of sight." Jules nods and tucks the large pistol under his leg. The two ride side-by-side onto the fort grounds and proceed past several large tents of merchants.

A pair of hard-looking men steps out of one of the canvas saloons and passes before Holton and Jules. The man in the lead glances up, showing a bloody wound stretching from his lower lip to a scabbed-over hole in his cheek. Jules nearly falls from the saddle pulling the Walker pistol from under his leg. He hastily pulls back the hammer and turns his horse to get in a better position to aim.

The action catches the corner of Holton's sightline, and he holds back his mount as he pivots in the saddle. Before he can reach out to stop the boy, there is a fiery discharge of the Walker pistol. The man next to the intended target falls back with a close range, bullet wound slammed into his chest.

The man with the scar across his cheek promptly recognizes Jules and pulls his pistol, firing and missing. Holton spurs his horse forward and charges into the man's extended gun arm, sending his second shot wild and tumbling him back. Another gunshot barks from the door of the tent saloon, and Holton wheels his mount as he draws his sidearm. He returns a pistol shot that rips through the canvas saloon door and sends the man ducking back inside.

Holton looks over at Jules and watches as the boy cocks his Walker pistol with both hands and charges his mount after the fleeing man with the facial scar. The boy gallops across the clearing at the center of the fort grounds after the man running afoot. The chase ends on the opposite side where they stop at the parked military wagons and horse corral. Holton steals a glance toward the saloon door again before yelling after Jules. "Dammit boy … Get back here!"

Dog darts under a nearby wagon to keep clear, and Holton snaps off another shot at the tent saloon. He spurs his horse after Jules across the parade grounds, and Dog follows after. They both race to the far side of the open field and encounter Jules, still horseback, aiming his pistol at the man with the cheek wound. Holton rides up and slide-stops his horse next to Jules. "Hold it there!"

The bloody-cheeked man backs up against the broad-side of a wooden wagon. He still holds a pistol, while raising his hands in surrender. "Mister, I don't even know this kid."

Jules looks passionately toward Holton, while the heavy weight of the extended gun barrel wavers. "He's a liar! He took my sisters!"

Dog barks, and Holton lowers his sidearm slightly, looking back toward the tent saloon. Several men scamper out the canvas flap door and dash for their horses. He turns to the surrendered man and studies the freshly scabbed over cheek and mouth injury.

"Who are you?"

"The name's Ben Sighold …"

A hint of recognition strikes Holton and Dog growls. "Bloody Ben?"

The sound of gunfire erupts from the recently mounted men nearby. Several shots whiz past and the hot smack of rifle lead grazes Holton's left shoulder. Bloody Ben ducks under the empty wagon behind him and rolls away, as the blast of the Walker pistol smashes through a wooden wheel spoke.

Holton turns and fires his pistol at the four men on horseback charging across the parade grounds toward them. He positions his mount protectively in front of Jules and slides his big-loop rifle from the saddle scabbard. One handed, he snaps off a shot from the rifle and twirl cocks the long-arm, ready to accept the assault.

Sinking his spurs in the horse's flank, Holton holds tight as his horse digs in and lunges forward. Surrounding the parade grounds, dozens of military troopers gather to the sounds of gunfire. Holton charges his horse ahead to violently meet the four horseback attackers.

After just a few leaps forward, the solid unforgiving buttstock of a Springfield rifle smashes into Holton's body and knocks him from his mount. Quickly surrounded by dismounted troops, Holton hits the ground with a thud. He looks around to see several rifles pointed down at him and Dog growling at the assembled soldiers.

Regaining his breath, Holton lies on the military parade field and lets his rifle and pistol fall from his grip. He looks back to where Jules was previously and can't make him out in the increasing crowd of blue military uniforms. "Easy Dog…" The canine stops his aggressive stance and slinks back.

A rifle jabs Holton along his wounded shoulder, and he looks up at the familiar, yet empty stares, of United States Army soldiers. One of the troopers hollers down at him. "Leave them guns and git to yer feet!"

Holton stands and watches, as the four horseback assailants who charged him ride away from the camp followed by another rider who is sure to be Bloody Ben. He quickly scans the fort grounds again for Jules, but the boy is nowhere in sight.

The arresting trooper jabs his rifle barrel firmly into Holton's ribs and growls, "Who ya lookin' for? There's no one here to help ya."

"There was a boy with me ..."

Another soldier turns his bayonetted long-arm sideways and shoves Holton forward, pushing him toward one of the wood framed buildings. "Tell it to the Major."

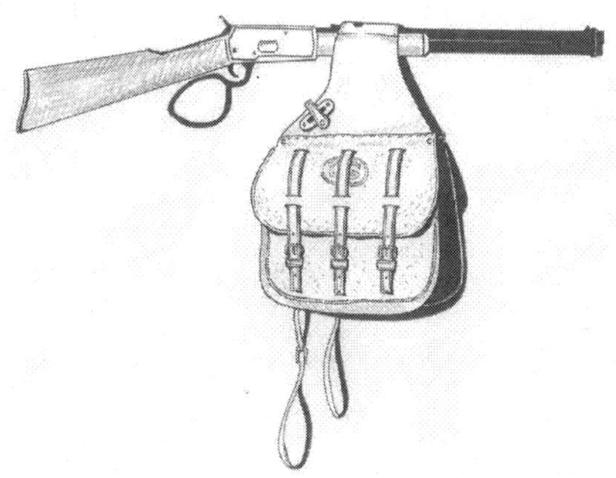

Chapter 10

To the east of Fort Tularosa, five horseback riders travel away at a hard gallop. Bloody Ben rides at the lead and looks back at the gang of four following him. The mismatched set of fleeing desperados consist of hard cases and rejects from all over the southwest territory.

A lean, wiry Mexican, by the name of Poncho Ruiz, squints from under his floppy felt sombrero. He has a narrow-eyed look and sun-creased wrinkles from years of outdoor living. Atop a spirited stallion, he wears stained leather-fringed britches that hang down over a set of fancy roweled spurs.

Beside Poncho rides a large, bearded man who owns the moniker 'Elephant-tooth Willie'. The distinctive name seems derived from the constant scowl formed by the incisor tooth that projects from the left side of his mouth. He carries a sawed-off shotgun across the pommel of his horse and, when the time is opportune, he is often quick to use it.

Not far behind them, Gimp Ear Walt, a tall skinny youth, wears a beat-down, felt top-hat that is crooked to the side to hide the jagged scar where his ear cartilage once was. He looks to the rider trailing behind and hurries his pace with the others to avoid riding beside the last one coming up.

At first glance, Snake-belly Sue appears to be a disagreeable looking man, but turns out to be an even uglier woman. Dressed in men's clothing, she has more guts and a hotter temper than most of the ruffians she runs with. Her muscled thighs squeeze against the saddle skirting, and she crowds her mount up on Gimp Ear Walt, enjoying the antagonizing effect on the youth.

Bloody Ben slows his horse along a less traveled path and raises his hand to signal the others to stop. His practiced demeanor and erect poise in the saddle is faintly reminiscent of military cavalry training. He wheels his horse around to address his followers.

"Hold up there boys."

Snake-belly Sue spits a long stream of tobacco juice and takes no affront to the suggestion of her gender. She brings her mount up alongside the others and wipes the dribble from her jowly chin. "What the hell was that about back there?"

Elephant-tooth Willie raises his shotgun to rest the stock on his thigh and glances over his shoulder at the others. "Which was the one who killed Karl? Was it the little boy or the Indian Scout?"

The trailing dust settles, and Bloody Ben Sighold listens into the far distance for anyone following before looking his remaining crew over. "It was the damned kid who shot me twice and jumped that cliff in Arizona."

The Mexican man, Poncho Ruiz crosses a spurred heel over his saddle pommel and laughs. "Mi amigo told you that niño had wings ..."

Snake-belly Sue grunts. "Damned unlikely. How do you know it was him?"

Ben glares at the disagreeable woman and tongues the ragged hole still healing through his cheek. "I'd recognize the business end of that boy's horse pistol anytime. If his animal hadn't of shimmied, he would have blasted me dead instead of Karl catching his lead." Poncho spins his spur rowel and shrugs. "Why you not jest shoot him this time?"

Ben turns his hard stare toward Poncho. "And have half that damn garrison out after us for killing a runt-ass kid?" The Mexican starts to smile. "I can go back tonight and slit 'is throat." Poncho points a finger and wipes it across his neck.

The gang leader smirks at the homicidal suggestion and looks out over their back trail toward the fort. "He'll be along soon enough. He followed us from Arizona didn't he?"

Snake-belly Sue scratches under her arm along her ribs like an animal with fleas. Her broken fingernails make a snagging sound on her wool weave vest. "I think it was that fella wearin' Injun buckskins, with the cur dog, who done most of the following."

Gimp Ear Walt shakes his head, worrisome, as he looks around at his outlaw partners and mumbles under his breath, "I don't like to be hunted by a dog."

They all peer over their shoulders toward their recent path and half expect to see a rider with a dog appear. Ben spurs his horse and turns it away from the afternoon sun. "Doesn't matter. We got work to do, and there's jest the two of 'em. You ever see that pair again, jest shoot 'em." Ben gives the sweated rump of his horse a slap and gallops away with the others following after.

~*~

Holton sits in an armless wooden chair in the middle of a sparsely furnished room. He wears iron wrist shackles connected to a chain that binds him to a metal ring attached to the floor. Out of his reach, on a table set across the room, sit his hat, rifle and holster belt.

The sounds of the fort activity outside come through a high, narrow window that lets in a hazy beam of sunlight. Holton waits quiet and tests the tightness of the metal cuffs. He gives a firm tug at the unyielding and secure chain anchored to the floor. A shuffle of feet outside the entryway catches his attention, and he glances over as a key in the mechanism unlocks, and the heavy door swings open.

A military-uniformed sergeant enters and strides across the room to the slab table containing Holton's possessions. He strikes a match and puts the flame to the charred wick of an oil lamp on the wall. The sergeant inspects the items on the table and lifts the big-loop rifle from the pile. He looks it over and struggles with the urge to spin the large lever before setting it down again.

Sergeant Kilbern turns to glare at the newly arrived prisoner chained in the room as the lamplight on half his face glows ominously. The disgruntled career military man seems bitter and resentful of his modest rank and overcompensates with aspiration of a more prestigious position. He studies Holton in the fading light from the window and glow of the lamp, then grumbles, "Holton Lang, you say yer name is?"

"Yes."

"Some say they've heard of you in Texas."

His chained wrists in his lap, Holton stares quietly at the uniformed soldier. The sergeant steps around the table and leans on the edge.

"I ain't heard of you."

"Some haven't."

"Give me a story of what happened today."

"I was unsaddled 'fore anything come about."

The sergeant clasps his hands together and walks closer. "What about the dead man?"

Holton stares ahead then peers up at the sergeant as the interrogator looms over him. "You should bury him."

"You shoot 'im?"

Holton looks away and stares at the mud brick wall. "Did he say I did?"

The sergeant reaches back and hammers a fist to Holton's jaw, turning him in the chair. "I won't tolerate no smart lip from you, half-breed. Folks say you're big shit in Texas, but you ain't there now." A trickle of blood shows at the corner of Holton's mouth.

He sucks the bloody inside of his cheek and spits to the floor. Their eyes connect, and the two stare at each other a long moment before Sergeant Kilbern turns and walks to the door. He looks back, and a hint of a cruel smile crosses his stern features. "Don't go anywhere... When the Commanding Officer returns from the field, there will be a short trial followed promptly by a hanging."

Chapter 11

The small hand of the boy traces the assortment of horse tracks leading east out of the fort. Jules kneels on the ground and studies the mixture of prints coming to and leaving the area. The boy shakes his head, frustrated, as he stands and takes up the reins to his mount. He stares at the ground, Walker pistol in one hand and the bridle reins in the other.

Not far away, concealed in the brush, the dark eyes of a canine watch as the boy gazes out to the wild terrain in the east and back to the canvas and smoke from the dwellings of the military encampment. Jules climbs the stirrups to his mount and eases into the saddle. He takes one last forlorn look to the broken trail leading away and turns the head of his horse back toward Fort Tularosa.

~*~

After traveling most of the day away from the fort, Bloody Ben and his riders return to their assorted plunder from the raids on homesteaders. The camp consists of two loaded wagons, a grouping of horses and a circle of female captives bound together near a spot of shade. The returning outlaws ride past the wagons, and Bloody Ben looks down at the knife-sliced and barely breathing form of a young woman alongside one of the spoked wheels. He steers his horse over to several gathered men in native leather buckskins, as they play cards on a homespun blanket.

"Dull Blade, what the hell is this?"

The following riders stop, and Ben gestures back to the sliced up and bloody figure on the ground. One of the foremost Indians sets his cards aside and rises. He stares at Ben and the riders without fear of reproach. "The girl bothered me with wailing."

Bloody Ben and the other riders look to the grisly site as the brutalized girl whimpers, half-alive. "Well, she will come out of yer cut of the sale." The native man, Dull Blade, smiles an evil grin and touches the handle of his sheathed knife, as he admires the result of his ghastly work. "I cut my share from her already."

Ben veers his mount back over to the horseback riders, as they look on, angered by the abuse of the valuable prisoner. He hollers over his shoulder for all the listening Indians to hear. "Don't nobody mess with the others, and we'll get good money from them yet."

With their horses idling by the wagons, Gimp Ear Walt looks ill at ease as he turns to Sue. "Best git them little gals sold 'fore that bloody savage carves 'em all up." In contempt, Sue spits a stream of tobacco juice aside and glares hard at Dull Blade as he returns to the card game. "I'd like to put my blade in that chicken-shit Injun." As Ben joins them, Walt looks around at his riding companions. "Nobody's stoppin' ya."

With a hissing whisper, Bloody Ben eyes his assembled gang. "Keep quiet you two! Let it stand for now. We got to expect to lose a few along the way." Snake-belly Sue growls and spits her chaw juice again. "He's cuttin' into what ain't his."

Ben heaves a snort and glances over his shoulder at the circle of gambling natives. His look of contempt and bigotry is obvious in his slanted glare. "Damn Injuns think everything is owed them." The sneering outlaw leader lifts a whiskey bottle from his saddle bag and smiles through his crusted cheek wound. "If I have it my way, none of this will be theirs. Hand me another bottle."

The four riders look around at each other and down at their overstuffed saddle pouches. The supply of several glass bottlenecks can be seen protruding from each bag. Irritated, Ben shakes his bottle and gestures to Walt. "Gol-dammit ... Gimp Ear, give me one of yourn."

"No sir! I only gots the two. Go n' git one from Elephant-tooth's stash."

Protective of his stock, Elephant-tooth Willie snarls at Walt and gives a cold stare toward Ben. The outlaw leader's sneer fades and his eyes blaze with an impatient, growing anger. "You damn nickel-carvers! I only had a chance to get this one potion from the post hospital 'fore Karl was killed. Give me a damn bottle, or I'll have you all in the mix."

Bloody Ben glares at his gang and is met by unyielding gazes from Snake-belly Sue, Elephant-tooth Willie, and Poncho. Gimp Ear Walt finally caves under Ben's ominous stare, reaches back and pulls a bottle from his leather horse pouch. "What do I get fer it?"

Ben grumbles under his breath as he sets one bottle in his lap and holds out his empty hand. "I don't let Snake-belly mount you in the night."

Gimp Ear looks over at Sue, and she makes a vulgar pumping of her arms. He tosses the whiskey bottle to Ben and steals a glimpse back at the rough, laughing form of Snake-belly Sue. Walt whimpers, as he tries to ignore the repulsive gestures of the sexually aggressive woman.

"Why don't she jest leave me alone? She ain't bothered you others none."

Poncho laughs his Mexican chortle as he leans a bent elbow back on his horse's rump. "She will ride you into the ground with her tender love and tear off your other ear!" The Mexican reaches his hand high, kicks his feet out from the stirrups and rides an imaginary bucking bronc.

The others laugh and watch, as Ben carefully pours the medicinal elixir into both the amber bottles of whiskey. He finishes off the mixture and gives the glass containers a swirl before shoving the corks back in. Bloody Ben looks up at the gang and stares them down with a wicked intent. "This ought to do the trick. Don't none of you share with that Injun or his braves if you want to keep on."

All around the outlaw group, they nod and look to the circle of gambling Indians gathered around Dull Blade. The hands of cards are laid out, and the entertained warriors squabble while collecting their bets. The muffled sound of their arguments resonates across the quiet camp.

~*~

Holton sleeps slumped uncomfortably in the ladder-back chair. He hears the scratching of small feet on the wall outside and looks through the high window up to the brightly colored evening sky. Patiently, he waits, as the climbing outside continues.

The sight of youth-sized fingers on the window ledge is followed by the tossing of a thick, metal Ferrier file that hits the hard-packed dirt floor with a *twang*. He looks to the floor and the serrated edge of the horseshoeing tool. Gazing back to the window, Holton watches, as the boy's hand gripping the windowsill gives a short wave and drops from view.

Holton listens awhile and hears the receding footsteps of Jules fade into the sounds of nightfall. He slides down in the creaking chair and reaches his booted foot out. Holton catches the edge of the object with his extended toe and drags the file blade closer. He nudges the metal cutting tool along the dirt floor and hears the faint murmur of voices outside. The loud, grinding sound of the door being unlocked forewarns him of a visitor.

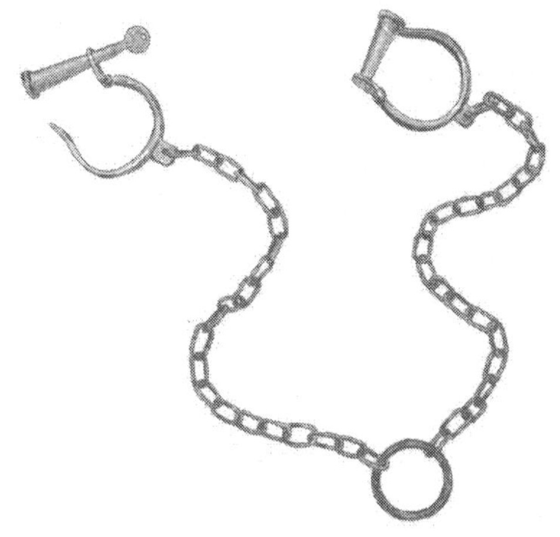

Chapter 12

The cooler air of dusk begins to drift in from the high window as the dim light darkens to night. The heavy door swings open, and Sergeant Kilbern steps inside. He slowly looks around the shadowed room, as the last hint of daylight filters in. With a quick glance over his shoulder, he shuts the door behind him.

Holton slowly places his foot over the file blade, as Kilbern walks toward him and circles. The sergeant studies the linked-chain shackles on the prisoner and speaks low. "You have a confession for me yet?"

"What about?"

Holton stares forward as the sergeant passes behind the chair and pauses. Ears perked, Holton's body slowly tenses as the presence of the military man behind him looms with hostility and talks in a husky whisper.

"Mister Holton Lang ... It would go much better for you if you concede that you killed that man."

"Why would I do that?"

Sergeant Kilbern swings out with his fist and hammers Holton on the back between the shoulder blades. Holton winces and flexes his spine. The sergeant leans down and pulls the buckskin clad prisoner back in the wooden chair. "Admit you killed that man!"

"It won't matter none in your court."

"You can swing by a rope as a coward or a man."

Holton shakes the officer's grip off his shoulder and glares back at the bullish interrogator.

"Which are you?"

Kilbern steps around to the front of the chained captive and punches his fist into Holton's abdomen. The sergeant snarls as he pulls his hand from Holton's bent over form.

"I'm the better man when it comes to you, Injun-lover."

Trying to catch his air, Holton raises his shackled hands to chest level. The chain strains against the anchor in the floor, and he looks through the metal links to Kilbern and growls, "This do make us about equals ..."

Sergeant Kilbern glares at the mixed-race American before him and rubs his clenched fist. "I bet you want me to give you the key to them irons and make this more interestin'? Kilbern makes a mocking show of empty pockets with his side-slit trouser pouches hanging out like rabbit ears. "Well Mister Lang, I don't got it ... Besides, I'm gonna enjoy watchin' yer murderin' neck stretched like the common Injun trash you are."

Dropping his hands to his lap, Holton lowers his gaze to the floor and Kilbern stoops to lean closer. The hot stale breath of the military man blows in the prisoner's downcast eyes. "You hear me red-skin?"

In a flash, Holton reaches out and grabs the sergeant by the collar and pulls him close. He twists the slack chain around Kilbern's neck and clamps down tight. Holton whispers in the man's ear as the sergeant claws at the cold iron links and gasps for air. "You ain't much of a man compared to most and, the next time you raise my dander, I'll kill ya."

Sergeant Kilbern gulps for breath with the unyielding chain links cinched around his neck, and his face flushes with strain. The military man slaps his hand on the floor, begging for mercy, just before he chokes out. Holton gives another quick squeeze and shoves him away.

Gulping for air, Kilbern scoots across the dirt floor, climbs to his knees and holds his red, shackle-marred neck. He looks back at Holton with even more contempt and hatred than before and wipes the tears from his bloodshot eyes. Kilbern tries to cough and wheezes through a sore windpipe. "You're nothing but a damn savage ..."

The sergeant rises to his feet and stumbles on weak legs to the doorway. He pulls the heavy door open and supports himself, feeling faint. Looking back once more, he exits with a feeble fit of coughing and a grinding lock at the keyhole.

Holton looks down at his scuffed boot still covering the file-blade near the base of the chair. He scoots it closer and bends down to pick it up. Feeling his thumb along the rough jagged edge of the metal bar, he takes a measured breath.

Using a skilled, deliberate stroke, he rubs the cutting groves across the hasp that connects the wrist shackles. He glances up to the dark window above, then to the thick wooden door closing off the room. With short, even strokes, he continues the soft rasping cut of metal on metal.

~*~

A day's travel from the fort, the marauders' camp is lit up by a large fire that blazes into the night sky. The wagon, with the hostages tied near, sits at the edge of the firelight. Bloody Ben and his crew sit and drink, watchful while Dull Blade holds a whiskey bottle high and screams into the starlit heavens. The sweat-glistened savage tosses the bottle to one of his braves and pulls out a long gleaming knife from his leather waist sheath.

"Give me another of them white-eye women. I want to make 'er scream with the flesh torn from her bones!"

Letting out a low growl, Snake-belly Sue moves to stand, as she slowly draws her own knife blade. Bloody Ben quickly reaches out and puts his hand to her lap. "Don't you make a move." Ben rises with his bottle of whiskey and takes a long swallow. Standing opposite the fire, he does a comical dancing jig for Dull Blade. The Indian laughs uproariously and points his knife at the bandit leader.

"You dance like fire-chicken!"

Ben continues to kick out his booted heels and hollers, "You scream out like sow in heat!"

The Indian leader gestures his shining blade at the starry sky and smiles amused. "Let me cut up one more. I will make it last all night."

Ben stops his dance and waves his bottle toward the hostages. "We will sell them girls for good money in Tejas."

Dull Blade spits and stabs his knife in the night air. "Them dirty Comanchero are nothing but dog trash!"

"But they pay well for uncut squaws, 'n make 'em last much longer than you."

The fierce Indian grins and twists his gleaming blade over the flames of the crackling fire. "Jest one more … or maybe I call you *Ol' Squaw-Ben* instead of Bloody Ben."

The narrow gaze of Bloody Ben seems to rise with a vicious rage in the fiery reflection off his slanted eyes. He speaks loudly to the Indian leader across the dancing flames. "No more captives … Cut on the one you started earlier."

The half-drunk Indians look over to the mutilated form barely alive just outside the light of the campfire. Dull Blade crinkles his face with displeasure. "No fun left in her anymore…"

Ben pulls another swig of whiskey that drips from his opened cheek wound and tosses the mostly empty bottle to Dull Blade across the fire circle. "Have another drink and be happy with what you got."

Dull Blade catches the tossed bottle and swirls the lighter colored liquid in the firelight. He takes a swallow and eyes Ben maliciously. "I think I call you *One-who-catches-bullet-in-teeth*!"

Tonguing the oozing wound in his cheek, Bloody Ben clenches his jaw. He controls his intensifying anger and watches one of the Indians with the opiate-mixed whiskey keel over, passed out. Another brave, with long twisted braids, grabs the bottle from him and takes a gulping swig.

Ben knowingly smiles at Dull Blade and retakes his seat near Snake-belly Sue. She hands him a fresh, uncorked bottle, and he murmurs to himself before taking a swallow.

"I'll call him *trash-that-cuts-up-little-girls…*"

The surrounding outlaws all sit and observe as the whiskey-drugged Indians imbibe and eventually pass out, one by one.

~*~

Inside the confinement room at the fort, Holton continues to cut at his shackles and flex the iron bonds for signs of weakness. Metal flakes drift to the floor, as the rasping file does its work. He looks up to the early hints of morning through the high window and redoubles his efforts.

Chapter 13

The brightness of the morning sun crests the surrounding hills of Fort Tularosa as Sergeant Kilbern marches across the empty parade grounds. He stops at the main wood-framed structure, looks over his shoulder with a paranoid glance, then opens the door and enters. A few moments later, a military sentry exits the building and walks the distance to the privy.

Sounds of the heavy door lock being opened catches Holton's attention, and he gives the shackles one last pass before tucking the metal rasp under his leg. He looks down at the shiny, near cut-through irons and conceals them in his lap. The door opens, and Holton recognizes the silhouette of his unfriendly visitor from the night prior. "Good morning, Sergeant."

Kilbern steps inside and closes the door behind him. "Not for you it ain't."

The sergeant walks to Holton and stares down at him. He is careful to stay back a few steps, out of arm's reach. The dark figure of the military man looks past the prisoner to Holton's guns and hat on the far table.

"Unlucky for you, the colonel is due back today." Sergeant Kilbern returns his attention to Holton, and his shadowed features grin down at the captive. "You're gonna do some horse-tradin', 'fore yer neck gets stretched."

Holton shifts in his chair to keep the nearly cut-through shackles concealed. He looks up and speaks low and calm. "Step a bit closer 'n I'll finish what I started on yours."

Kilbern instinctively puts his hand to his bruised neck, pulls his shirt collar up and takes another step back. He travels a wide circle around Holton and picks up the big-loop rifle from the table. He levers the gun quietly, feeling the action before looking back at its owner. "This was the prize in a special shootin' contest, eh? It occurred to me that this unique rifle of yours might be worth a fair 'mount of money to some."

Sergeant Kilbern holds the esteemed big-loop trophy rifle across his chest and quickly aims it toward the morning light through the small window. "I heard some unbelievable stories and tall tales about how you supposedly won it in Texas a few years back."

The military man points the barrel around the dark room, lowering his aim to the back of Holton's head. He pulls the trigger to an empty click and sets the unloaded gun on the table behind him.

"Now, I can't steal it, but if you were to give it to me as a goodwill gesture, I wouldn't refuse it." From inside his coat pocket, the sergeant pulls two pieces of folded paper and opens them. Silently, he reads the writing over and smiles. He lays the creased sheets out on the table and puts pen to paper, signing Holton's name on both. "Signed by Holton Lang…"

His back to Sergeant Kilbern at the table, Holton peers down at the near cut-through shackles and strains against the unwieldiness of the bonds. He glances over his shoulder at the uniformed man, as he continues trying to break the uncut section of his shackles.

"The rifle is all you want?"

Kilbern refolds one piece of paper into his pocket and places the other on the table under Holton's hat. He lifts the rifle from the table, examines it with delight and glances to Holton. "Watching a half-breed, murderin' Injun hang will be a nice addition to the prize."

Sergeant Kilbern walks a wide circle around Holton and stops with his hand on the handle of the door. The rifle held at his side, the military man puts it comfortably over his shoulder. He turns and gives a contented glare at the man shackled to the middle of the floor.

The early light of day begins to fill the chamber, and the sergeant pulls open the heavy, iron-hinged door. The door creaks as Sergeant Kilbern exits the threshold, and a sound comparable to a wooden bat cracking a fresh melon is heard. The sergeant back-peddles, as he stumbles into the room with a flattened nose, gushing blood.

Kilbern finally catches his footing, when he bumps into the solid table. Holton watches as the special big-loop rifle falls from the sergeant's grip and tumbles to the hard-packed dirt floor with a rattle. Wavering on his feet, Kilbern turns to Holton as his eyes go crossed, and he slumps in a heap.

Holton turns to the doorway and heaves a relieved sigh when young Jules Ward steps into view. The boy holds the Mexican's Sharps rifle by the barrel like a club, along with the string of keys for the locks and shackles. Jules sets the rifle by the door and rushes over to unlock Holton. The boy fumbles with the turnkey and finally unfastens both iron handcuffs.

"Morning, Mister Lang."

"Hey, kid ..."

Free of the shackles, Holton rubs his sore wrists and looks down at Sergeant Kilbern, who lies prone on the dirt floor. A small trickling stream of fresh blood flows from the unconscious man's nose onto the hard-packed floor. Holton nods his head and looks to Jules. "Heck of a job, kid. Could he recognize your face?"

"Naw, was aiming for his ear when he turned into it."

Holton leans down and feels under Kilbern's jawline for a beating pulse. Satisfied that he is still alive, the two drag the sergeant nearer to the center of the room and fasten the shackles to his limp wrists. With the unconscious sergeant seated on the floor, they prop him up against the chair and the blood from his nose dribbles down his chin.

Jules watches inquisitively, as Holton tosses the bundle of keys out the high window. The buckskin clad westerner then smiles, amused, as he puts the metal file-blade within easy reach. Jules looks up to Holton and questions the deliberate placement of the cutting tool.

"What'll that do?"

"Make me feel better ..." Holton steps to the table, grabs up his age-worn cavalry hat and buckles on his gun belt. He lifts the big-loop rifle from the hard-packed earthen floor and blows the dirt from along the receiver's side. He pulls down the front brim of his hat like a salute and nods toward Sergeant Kilbern sprawled unconscious against the chair. "Adios, Sergeant."

Jules grabs up the Mexican studded Sharps rifle by the door and steps outside. Holton watches the young boy's exit and follows him. A strange surge of father-like pride sweeps over Holton, as he observes Jules carrying himself with integrity and confidence.

The oddly matched pair step outside the military building, as the early sun shines bright over the distant hills. Jules quietly ushers Holton around to the back, revealing their saddled horses tethered and waiting. The boy unties the leather reins, climbs a wood crate and leaps into the saddle.

Without a word, Holton nods his approval and seems impressed with the effective rescue as he steps off the porch onto the back of the other mount. A look of mutual respect and appreciation is exchanged between them, as they continue on their quest. They both put heels to hide and lope their mounts around the far side of the military structure.

In the early light of day, the two horseback riders trot across the fort grounds. They pass the outdoor privy as a young soldier steps out while readjusting his gear. Holton gives a friendly salute, and the young man instinctively returns the gesture. The uniformed private watches the man and boy as they canter away then does a double-take to the fort structure containing the lockup.

~*~

Moving out in the morning sun, headed to the east, Holton and Jules ride toward Texas. Suddenly, Jules pulls up his mount to a skidding stop, stares ahead and looks over his shoulder back in the direction of Fort Tularosa. Holton reins in to a slowing trot and circles back to look at the boy. "You forget something?"

"Nope … but what about them?" Jules gestures to a company of mounted US Cavalry coming over the rise on their same path, headed to the fort.

"Those are soldiers coming, Mister Lang."

"I seen 'em." Holton watches the column of horseback troopers as they snake the trail down the faraway hillside. Jules draws his Walker pistol from his saddlebag and holds it across his lap. Holton shakes his head and points at the large handgun. "Put that thing away. You ain't gonna fight 'em all."

"Won't they question us?"

"For what purpose? They're just returning after a long patrol. Not a one of 'em knows who we are."

Jules takes a moment to think it out and understand the explained reasoning. He tucks the horse pistol back in the saddle pouch and kicks his horse forward at a loping trot past Holton. The experienced westerner smiles to himself, catches up to pat the boy on the shoulder, then murmurs low, "Yer a smart one, but still need a lesson in jail breaks."

Jules looks up at Holton and shrugs. "I think I did pretty well for my first one."

"Not bad, kid … not bad t'all."

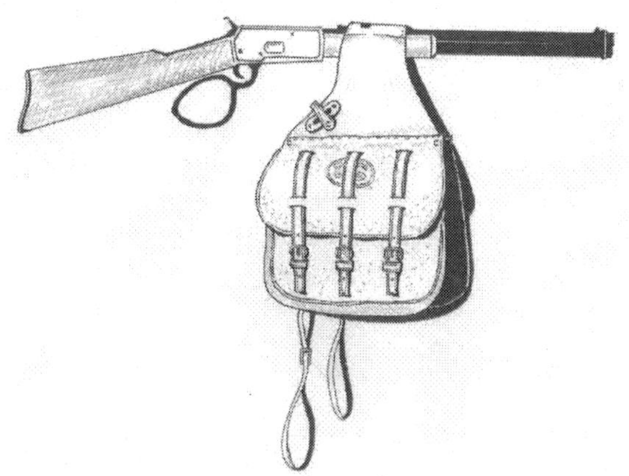

Chapter 14

Holton and Jules walk their horses along the trail and move away to the side, under sparse shade, as the column of cavalry troopers approach. The rattle and creak of military saddle tack and hooves clopping sound in unison as the unit nears. At the forefront of the group, a burly man with a bushy beard and sweat-stained buckskin shirt glances at the two riders.

The broad-chested man has the look of a life-long cavalry scout and Indian fighter. His rough, grizzled appearance is partly due to the completed patrol, though it doesn't seem to improve much when back to the home comforts of the fort. He sits atop a stout Indian pony and peers curiously over at the strangers.

Set back a ways from the main trail, Holton and Jules stand their horses in the shadows of a twisted cedar. They keep their mounts in check and avoid engaging with the eye-line of the troopers. The warming rays of the morning sun increase, as the unit of US Cavalry steadily trots past. Breaking to the side, but still moving along with the flow of riders, the cavalry scout observes the pair with a studious eye.

He has a sudden pang of recognition and inhales to yell out, when he chokes on the juicy cut of chaw in his cheek. The burly man roars with a hacking growl, making a dramatic scene as he coughs and spits out the wad of tobacco. His unchecked mount takes the lead from the loose reins and assumes the pace of the horses traveling alongside.

Several more throaty barks and the cavalry scout finally makes a recovery with a flushed demeanor. He wipes the dark tobacco dribble from the front of his leather shirt and turns in the saddle, as the two riders, man and boy, move off down the ranks of soldiers. Standing in the stirrups, he bellows out, "Holton Lang!!"

Halfway down the column of troops, Holton's ears prick at the thunderous calling of his name. He feigns not to hear and continues riding after the boy, while concealing any outward reaction or response. The traveling pair rides clear, past the line of troopers, and Holton controls his urge to look back toward the familiar-sounding voice.

The trail before them unobstructed, Holton ushers Jules on to a trotting lope up the next rise. At the top of the berm, Jules looks behind and studies the mounted cavalry troops through a haze of trail dust. "I heard your name back there?"

"Yeah, let's git ..."

The two continue away on the trail as the seasoned military scout, Bear Benton, peels off from the column of troopers and watches them ride over the distant hill.

~*~

Several fires still smolder around the marauder's camp, as the morning hours begin to wane. In the clearing, Bloody Ben stands and looks around the filthy heaps of drunken bodies, sprawled in slumber. Several of his gang members lay wherever they passed out, alongside the drugged renegade Indians. Ben walks over and gives the sleeping Gimp Ear Walt a kick in the rump. "Gimp Ear ... git yerself up."

Walt instantly sits up erect and looks around blankly, wide-eyed. He looks over at Snake-belly Sue, snoring loud not too far from him, and gives an involuntary shiver. "Yeah Ben, what's up?"

"Rouse the others. We're leaving."

In sleepy confusion, Gimp Ear Walt looks at Ben. He watches the outlaw leader step over Elephant-tooth Willie and pause. Ben turns and gives the heavy-breathing gang member a booted punt to the gut. The big man lets out a groan, coughs and sputters awake. Ben looks down at the snaggletooth thug and barks, "Git all them girls loaded in one of the wagons. Everything else we can load in the other."

Poncho Ruiz rises to an elbow and looks around the quiet encampment. The shade begins to recede, and the sun begins to shine down moving on toward midday. He rubs his throbbing temples, looks to the whiskey bottle next to him and lifts the cork. After a long swallow, the Mexican gives a shaking shudder and rumbles his whiskey tasting lips, "Mmm ... hair of the dog."

At the grouping of animals, Ben begins to saddle his waiting horse. He secures the cinch strap and looks around, momentarily, to see that all his outlaw followers have roused and the drugged Indians are still soundly passed out. His ragged cheek scab crinkles to form a smile as he turns back to assembling his saddle gear.

~*~

Traveling east, Holton rides alongside Jules, keeping his eyes steady and watchful on the trail ahead. The boy squints and tries to make out anything in the far distance. Jules watches the empty path before them a long while and finally can't resist inquiring, "Indians?"

Holton looks over at Jules questioningly.

"How's that?"

"Do you see something up there on the trail?

"No, I feel it mostly."

"What is it?"

"Someone is following us."

The boy turns in the saddle and looks around at the unoccupied trail behind. "I don't see anything back there."

Holton gives a slight shake of his head. "Nope."

Jules turns forward and glances at his riding companion. "How can you figure someone is following without ever lookin' back?"

Holton nods forward to the vegetation ahead, down the path. "No ... Following in the lead..."

Jules seems confused as Holton puts his ear to the wind then sniffs. The young boy riding alongside nearly startles from the saddle with fright when Holton gives a shrill, signal whistle and calls out, "Dog …?"

There is a rustle of the low bushes ahead, and the loyal mongrel steps from the scrub looking rangier than ever. Dog sits alongside the trail, peering up at the approaching riders. Holton stops his mount next to the waiting animal and looks down at the patient beast. They exchange a look of mutual understanding, and the man nods to his canine friend. "It's alright Dog, nothin' you could have done there."

Dog lets his mouth open with a smiling pant and wags his tail.

The boy sits on his horse watching, as Holton continues to ride on, with the dog following close behind the horse's heels at a nimble gait. Jules urges his mount up next to Holton and looks down at the following canine. "Mister Lang, what kind of dog is that?"

"He's an Indian sniffer."

"What's that?"

Holton glances over and smirks. "He'll sniff out an Indian at two miles."

"Really?"

"That's how he found me."

The boy looks back at Dog, who peers up and seems to grin. "Yer kidding?" Jules stares at Holton awhile and studies him for some kind of jest. "I never seen you feed him, why'd he come back?"

"He does as he pleases."

The two are quiet suddenly as Jules feels a sharp pang of familial loss. The boy stifles a sniffle and glances back at the dog. "My Paw used to call that independent."

"He is that. A good tracker and fighter, too…"

Holton glances over and senses the boy's need for comfort. An uneasy feeling surges over the man, and he turns ahead to give the boy his privacy. The two travel along silent awhile, before Holton resumes the discourse. "Ne'er know when I'll have to eat 'im though." The buckskin-clad westerner half grins and watches as the boy turns to Dog, concerned.

"You wouldn't eat Dog, would ya?"

"Ya got to catch 'im first."

Jules looks to Holton, narrows his eyes and shakes his head disbelievingly. A quiet whimper of a laugh comes from the boy, and the pair continues down the trail with Dog following.

Chapter 15

The heat of the sun is full past midday as the gang continues loading the captive girls and supplies into the two wagons. Bloody Ben stands on watchful guard with his rifle cradled in his arm, observing the preparation. He looks down at the former Indian partners, still unconscious, and sniggers under his breath to himself.

Gimp Ear Walt approaches the outlaw leader and looks around nervously at the sleeping bodies. "What's Dull Blade 'nd his braves gonna do when they wake up, and we're all gone?"

Ben shifts the weight of the rifle in his arms and stares at the one-eared bandit. He spits, as he walks over to one of the renegade Indians called 'Snake Foot' and holds his rifle over the sleeping brave's head. "Wakey, wakey little Snakey…" The drugged Indian continues to sleep soundly, and Ben smashes the rifle butt into the man's skull, crushing it like a grape. He slams the rifle down several more times, and the man's features disappear into a dampened pile of gore.

Gimp Ear Walt slowly shies away as his insides churn up a watery vomit taste. Bloody Ben stands over the dead Indian victim and lets the bloody stock end of the rifle drip. He gives it a shake and watches the lifeblood run out of the headless form into the dry sandy ground. All the assembled outlaws pause to watch, and Ben speaks to them without having to raise his voice. "Get everything you can into those wagons. Take the girls and loot, sell 'em across the Mexican border and meet me by the canyons of the Brazos."

The gang leader takes a few steps over to the wagon containing the female prisoners and eyes them purposefully. He selects three of them and pushes them into a separate grouping. Ben turns his gaze to Walt, as the ill-at-ease outlaw continues to stare in shock at the featureless body in the middle of the encampment.

"Saddle some Indian ponies for these. I'm gonna give them to the Comanchero as a present."

Gimp Ear nods quickly and scurries away to gather saddle horses, while the others continue to load both the hitched wagons.

Snake-belly Sue marches across the camp, past the headless, quivering form. She stands over Dull Blade as he lies passed out, whiskey-drugged in the sun. Ben watches her and grins knowingly. "What's on yer mind, Sue?"

She glances over at Ben and flashes a nasty smile. "They all fair game like that one?"

Bloody Ben wipes the dripping mess of brain matter off his rifle butt onto the dead Indian's shirt. "Have at 'em ..."

The hard-looking woman nods and steps closer to the prone figure of the renegade chief. She draws the warrior's skinning knife from the sheath at his side and lets it glimmer in the bright sun. The sharp reflection flashes on the sleeping Indian's features, but his eyelids remain closed in blissful obliviousness.

Snake-belly Sue calls out an Indian war-whoop and reaches down to lift Dull Blade's loin wrap. One hand reaches down to take hold and, with the knife, the other makes a sweeping cut. The observing outlaws in camp all wince in horror as Snake-belly Sue brings up the bloody male parts of Dull Blade and waves them around like a party toy. She laughs as she stands over the unconscious man with his male apparatus separated. "This'll teach the red devils to cut on little girls!"

Sue wipes Dull Blade's bloodied knife on his shoulder length hair and struts away with the flaccid trophy in one hand and his blade in the other. She walks to one of the larger trees surrounding camp and looks back at the others stealing sickened glances at her. Snake-belly Sue holds the limp piece of flesh against the trunk of a tree and pierces it with the Indian's skinning knife, pinning it on display. Everyone stares with astonished disgust, as she turns to the camp with a proud stance. "Any you other cock-danglers want to mistreat womenfolk that'a way, and I'll do ya the same."

Poncho Ruiz stands nearby behind the wagon with Elephant-tooth and whispers under his breath, "Anyone to do such a deed is no fit to be around."

Elephant-tooth Willie whistles low then self-consciously adjusts himself in his dirty trousers under his gun belt. He stares at the object pinned to the tree and then the castrated body still sleeping unawares. The large man gulps and shakes his thick head. "She sure didn't like that damn Injun."

The Mexican bandit looks at the large brute with a show of mock surprise. "You think so?"

Everyone resumes their tasks, and Bloody Ben looks to Gimp Ear Walt as he meekly brings over a saddled mount. He observes, amused, as the one-eared youth walks a wide circle around the malicious woman.

"Alright y'all, shows over!" yells Ben. "Sue, get them wagons loaded and move out. Do what ya want with 'em but make sure you kill all these redskins 'fore you hit the trail."

Gimp Ear Walt returns to finish tacking the other mounts, as Bloody Ben steps into the saddle. In a soldierly fashion, the bandit leader sits erect in the saddle and looks around at the untidy mess of a camp. He ushers the three young hostages toward Walt at the pony herd and, with pleading, horrorstricken gazes, they whimper softly, as they look back to the other captured females.

~*~

The day wears on, as Holton and Jules ride a narrowing trail that veers off to the southeast. Dog lopes ahead in the lead, like a knowing guide. The searching pair of man and boy ride alongside another, occasionally glancing down to the traveled path of partially-concealed sets of overlapping wagon and horse tracks.

Jules adjusts his small hind-end on the leather seat of the creaking saddle. He sits astride with the long barrel of the oversized Walker pistol tucked under his leg. "You think we'll catch up to them today?"

Holton glances over and nods solemnly. They are both silent awhile, until Holton finally speaks. "We'll find them alright, but there's no telling what we may be up 'gainst when we do."

Jules thinks about the looming encounter, and his features display an anxious concern for the outcome. "What will we do when we find them?

Holton looks up at the midday sun passing through a cloud. "We'll have to decide that when the time comes."

The boy rides quietly until morbid thoughts escape from his lips. "You think my sisters are still…?"

"There's no gain to sell 'em otherwise." Holton looks over at the young boy riding next to him and takes a deep measured breath before speaking. "If you want, I can continue this hunt on my own. This is a dangerous path we're on. I can deal with these types of men 'n try to bring back yer kin."

Jules' features turn rigid, and any fearful thoughts are chased away as his small hand goes to the handle of the big Walker pistol. "Will you kill all of 'em who done this?"

Holton glances down at the revenge-filled youth. "I'll do my best to get your sisters."

Jules shakes his head determined. "If you ain't gonna do them murderers right and give 'em what they got comin', then I'll just continue on."

Holton watches as Dog trots ahead then pauses to look back before continuing on. The seasoned westerner looks down at the youth next to him, with his short legs and booted feet dangling above the stirrups. He looks to the boy's hand clutched on the old-fashioned cap-and-ball firearm. "Sure is a lot of killin' for a young lad not full-grown yet. That sort of work will stay with you for life."

Jules looks up at Holton with a mournfully serious glare. "This sort of thing already has."

Holton holds up his horse and motions for Jules to halt his mount. They both sit quiet a moment and seem to know the other's thoughts. Reluctant to giving some sort of fatherly advice, the man speaks tenderly to the youth. "These types we're after are hard, vicious men who will kill as soon as they set eyes on you again."

"And I will do the same for them."

He looks down at the boy and senses his loss of innocence. "I've grown fond of you … I would hate to see you get hurt in all of this."

Jules Ward looks at Holton with an acquired maturity well beyond his years. "I value your concern for my welfare, Mister Lang, but I am going to kill those men and get my sisters back … or die trying."

The two stare at each other, with the quiet surrounds of nature seeming to freeze in time. They both hesitate, not sure of what will happen or how to proceed next. Holton thinks on his next words carefully, when a piercing cry of agonizing pain echoes out from a few miles distant.

Dog stands in the wagon tracks with a poised stance, listening ahead and standing by. Holton reaches down and draws his big-loop rifle from the saddle scabbard. He gives the long-arm a twirl-cock and holds his horse at the ready.

"That yonder wail is likely from their camp. Git that horse pistol in hand and keep beside me." Holton looks down at the boy's oversized handgun. "Don't hammer off a shot 'till you know sure you can drop one. You'll only get one chance at 'em!"

Jules pulls the Walker pistol from under his leg and gathers up his reins as he watches Dog race away down the trail. Holton glances at the revenge-filled boy and gives an assertive nod. Spurs clench, Holton leaps his horse forward, followed by Jules and his ready mount. The two gallop down the trail, where the wails of distress from afar echo with an agonizing dreadfulness.

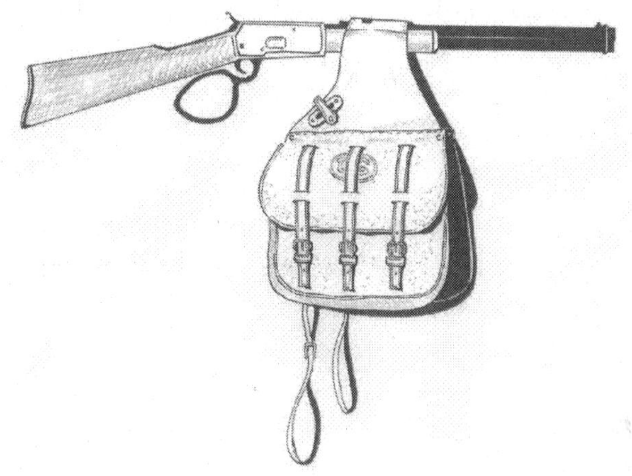

Chapter 16

The cries of anguish reverberate through the outlaw camp as Dull Blade stumbles around searching in vain. Red smears of blood cover his hands and run down the insides of his thighs. He falls to the ground and crawls feebly while wailing over his loss. The others find the scene disturbing, but Snake-belly Sue stops her task at hand and laughs uproariously at the bloody Indian searching for his missing parts. "What happened, Chief? Ya lose something?"

Poncho ties his saddled horse to the back of the loaded supply wagon and climbs into the driver's box. The dreadful howls continue, and he looks beyond the wagon's cargo to Dull Blade skulking in a drunk, half-dazed haze. Poncho shakes his head and mumbles low. "Somebody shoot that poor wretch already…"

At the other wagon, Elephant-tooth Willie ties down the canvas tarpon to shade the hostage women. Gimp Ear Walt sits atop his horse and tries not to look at Dull Blade's organ stuck through with a knife blade on the nearby tree. The outlaw covers his good ear while his gaze travels overpoweringly to the butchered man-parts, and he finds that watery bile taste in his mouth again.

The wailing screams from the wounded chief wake one of the other renegade Indians. The lethargic brave sits up and crawls through the camp on his knees. His long braids hanging low, the brave stops at the recently murdered companion with the smashed head. The confused Indian stares a long while and looks up to the wagons loaded with the hostage women and mercantile.

The roused native sits back on squatted haunches and tries to clear his blurred vision and drug-muddled thoughts. The outlaw gang continues with their departing chores, unaware of the awakened Indian digesting the scene. Wincing into the sun, the conscious brave starts to call out, when a rifle bullet tears through his chest, tumbling him back.

Snake-belly Sue steps up holding her recently-fired rifle and begins to laugh maniacally. She blows the smoke from the end of the barrel and kicks the shot Indian with her boot. The injured brave writhes in the dirt next to the head-smashed victim, and she giggles as she looks down at Bloody Ben's prior effort.

In reaction to the unexpected gunshot, Gimp Ear Walt nearly jumps out of his skin. He holds his startled horse in check and blurts out in a high pitched whimper, "Damn, Sue, what the hell!"

The female butcher gleams up at Walt and winks. "Ol' Ben told us to take care of these savages!" She chambers another cartridge into her rifle and shoots the dying man in the head as he squirms on the ground.

Moving to the next sleeping Indian, Sue nudges him over with her boot and puts the muzzle of the long gun under his nose. The awakened warrior slowly opens his eyes and stares blankly up at the hard-featured woman. She smiles her toothy grin and squeezes back the trigger.

The others keep their distance from the slaughter-happy she-bandit, as she seems to enjoy the pitiless task. Poncho takes up the reins of the mule team and turns away with obvious disgust.

"Is good ... you take care of the filthy work." Poncho looks back at Willie, who shrugs and hoists himself onto the other wagon with the female hostages. The blast of the gunshots begins to wake the other slumbering braves, and Sue levers her rifle in stride.

Suddenly the slight reverberation of galloping horses approaching is felt, and Poncho holds up his hand for silence. The others don't seem to notice, and the Mexican calls out, "Hold it! Someone is coming..."

Snake-belly and the others turn to Poncho and listen. Gimp Ear Walt nudges his horse over and turns his good ear out to take note of the distinct sound of pounding hooves. He looks around at the others and shrugs innocently. "It could be Ben coming back with them gals?"

Poncho slowly shakes his head. "No es Ben."

While seated on the wagon, Poncho draws his pistol from the holster at his hip. He looks around and tries to listen while Dull Blade continues to wail and cry for his lost manhood. The Mexican points his gun at the senseless Indian and hisses, "Shut that one up so's I can hear!"

There is a hush over the outlaws as the Indians slowly stir awake, and Dull Blade continues to yelp in manic disbelief of his physical state. The ground trembles, and the rumble of approaching hooves increase. Finally, the horseback forms of Holton and Jules burst from the brush into the scene of the renegade camp. Their mounts whirl and spin, as gunshots instantly explode from both sides.

Atop the driver's box, Poncho takes a shot with his pistol and dives away over the side of the wagon. Holton fires at him with his rifle, and the bullet smashes through the backrest of the wooden bench in an explosion of splinters. Gimp Ear Walt shoots his pistol twice before his horse bucks him off. He tumbles to the ground, then, on his knees, scrambles away into the brush.

Jules' horse circles wildly, as the boy tries to direct his aim. He fires a single shot, missing wide of Elephant-tooth Willie. The large man slaps the reins on the mule team, and the wagon jerks forward. Willie picks up his double-barreled shotgun, lays it over his arm and lets go with the right chamber toward Jules.

The buckshot tears into the boy's spinning horse and drops them to the ground. Jules rolls free of the fallen animal and holds his oversized pistol tight. He runs through the crazed activity of the camp and tries to intercept Elephant-tooth Willie and the hostage wagon as it turns to depart down the trail.

Horseback in the middle of the action, Holton spin-cocks his rifle and fires at Snake-belly Sue, as she raises her gun toward him. His shot tears into the stock near the lever and rips two fingers from her right hand. She howls like a wounded bear, grabs at the pistol in her belt with her uninjured hand and goes for cover.

Another twirl-levering of the big-loop rifle and Holton observes the boy running after the hostage wagon. He spurs his horse forward to block their exit and turns the wagon team back into the area of the camp. One handed, he extends his rifle arm and fires a shot that buries itself into the torso of Elephant-tooth Willie.

Groaning with a bullet sunk in his chest, Willie holds the shotgun close and slumps over the driver's box. With the reins held taut on the left mule, the team circles, almost running over Jules, who dives clear of the skittering hooves and crushing wheels. The boy rolls away and quickly hops to his feet with the Walker pistol in hand.

Poncho unties his saddle horse from the back of the other wagon and swings into the high cantle, rawhide seat. A bloody hand paws at his leg and he wheels his horse around. He kicks Snake-belly Sue away, while she clings to his stirrup. "Git yer own horse, you gutter slut!"

"Help me, Poncho … me hand's all shot to hell."

"Serves you right." The Mexican continues attempting to kick the hysterical woman away from his mount, while she grasps at him with her bloody three-fingered hand. Finally, he lowers his cocked pistol toward her and fires point-blank into her temple. The back of her head explodes out, and she quickly drops to the ground in a heap. Poncho sinks his large, roweled spurs into the horse's flanks, and the animal screams as it lunges away from the fighting action.

Having eyes on the fleeing Mexican, Holton halts his steed and draws a bead on Poncho. An anticlimactic cartridge misfire delays his opportunity, and he twirl-cocks a fresh round into the chamber. His second shot is sent askew by the wailing Dull Blade, who blindly stumbles into Holton's mount, letting Poncho disappear into the cover of the scrubby trees.

The hostage wagon continues to circle, and Jules stands his ground as it comes around. Elephant-tooth Willie holds his shotgun and steers the slow-charging wagon directly at the young boy. Jules cocks his piece, raises the pistol with both hands and fires. The .44 caliber bullet clips the big man's brainpan, pushing his hat back with a load of skull fragments.

As the mule team eases to a walk, Elephant-tooth Willie looks up and tries to speak. He puts his hand over the gaping head wound and sputters, "You tried to kilt me, boy ..." He levels the shotgun at the youth as Jules tries to pull back the hammer of the large pistol again.

Holton turns and watches, too late, as both firearms explode in a cloud of black powder smoke. He jabs his horse toward the standoff, as Jules spins to the ground with several shotgun pellets to his left side. Elephant-tooth Willie kneels forward in the wagon, struck dead with a bullet to his heart.

Slide-stopping his mount and leaping from the saddle, Holton kneels down and scoops the youth up in his arms. He sees several bloodied spots on Jules' shirt and trousers, and whispers calmly, "Where you hit, boy?"

Jules winces and struggles to catch a glimpse of the large outlaw slumped in the wagon. "I ain't killed…" Holton looks Jules over quickly and sees about a half dozen pellet wounds on the young boy's left side and arm.

The wailing calls of Dull Blade turn them back to the lulled action and a count of the dead. Holton stands with his rifle and waits as the bloody renegade Indian stumbles at him. He quickly sidesteps the feeble charge and smashes the crazed Indian with the stock of his gun. Another tap of the rifle barrel across the Indian chief's crown knocks Dull Blade unconscious to the ground.

The air is heavy with spent powder smoke and the encampment is deathly still, with exception of the bawling moans of Jules' dying horse. Holton steps over and puts the muzzle of his rifle to the animal's head. The blast of a gunshot echoes through the rolling hills, and all is quiet.

Chapter 17

A small unit of US Cavalry rides out of Fort Tularosa with Sergeant Kilbern at the lead. The troopers ride in two short columns, side by side, with the red over white, swallow tail cavalry guidon flag popping overhead in the wind. The sergeant has a stern, determined look about him, offset by his busted nose and two blackened eyes.

~*~

On the trail east of the Texas border, Bloody Ben leads the three captive girls mounted on Indian ponies.

He peers over his shoulder and listens for anyone following his back-trail. The sight of the man's profile with the ragged hole through his cheek turns the hostages away with fright. Ben scowls and tongues the raw inside of his mouth before turning in the saddle, prodding his horse and jerking the lead line.

~*~

Holton stands looking down at Jules who is laid on a spread-out blanket, with the liberated hostage women tending to his multiple wounds. The boy regains consciousness and looks up to the unfamiliar faces of the various females. He looks around for his sisters and grimaces in pain. "Where are Mary Beth and Annie?"

The four women continue bandaging the boy's wounds and look grim. Jules struggles to push them away and sits up. He looks around the camp, then toward Holton. "My sisters, where are they!"

Holton holds his big-loop rifle across his lap and squats low next to the boy. "They said Bloody Ben took three from the group and left an hour or two before we arrived."

Jules looks to his numerous bandaged wounds and pushes to his feet. The women watch the strong-willed boy rise, and they remain at the ready with their primitive medical supplies. He takes a step and winces. "Let's git after them…"

The pain of his wounds is too much; Jules becomes faint and falls back. The young women cradle the boy in their arms and ease him back to the blanket. Holton shifts his weight on his haunches and looks over at Jules. "We can go after them as soon as you're mended."

"I can go now..." Jules tries to sit up again but stops, woozy. The concerned mentor watches the young man and feels a sharp tinge of guilt for leading the youth into danger. "Them's only shotgun pellets on the surface, but at closer range things would've been different."

Jules grimaces sorely and tries to hold back the flowing tears as the girls resume cleaning and wrapping his wounds. "Did we get them others?"

"The Mex shot one of his own, and you took care of the big guy in the wagon." Holton glances down at the Walker pistol, still clutched firmly in the boy's small hand. "One fella dashed off as we arrived and some of them renegade Apache are dead, but it wasn't our doing." The buckskin man gestures over to the assembled Indians. "Them others remaining are mostly still loopy and put out on opiates."

Holton stands and Jules looks over toward the three captured Apache with their hands bound behind, near the wagon wheel. "Can't we just shoot them?" Feelings of shameful remorse swell over Jules as soon as the vengeful thought escapes his lips.

The half-breed scout stares down at the boy quietly a moment then speaks. "We won't be executing anyone. Things happen in a fight, but taking a man's life is no light doing."

The boy nods ashamed and glances to the prisoners. "What do we do with them?"

Holton runs his finger across his mouth and shrugs. "We'll have to take these stolen women along with the Apache prisoners back to Tularosa. They can deal with them there and git the girls to their families."

"That would be taking us in the wrong direction."

"For us it would, not for them."

The encampment is suddenly put on guarded alert when the sharp earsplitting shriek of an Indian war call pierces the air. Everyone turns, as the sinister form of Dull Blade rises from the ground, covered in dried, blackish blood from the waist down. He continues his war scream, as he stumbles to one of his dead companions and grabs up a pistol from the ground.

Calling out a haunting death chant, he charges at Holton with the handgun raised. He pulls the hammer and clicks two empty chambers on the revolver before a rifle bullet zings from the brush thickets behind and topples the renegade Apache chief at Holton's feet. Everyone gapes down at the dead Indian, still in shock from the fleeting event.

Holton turns his rifle aim and looks to the source of the shot from the scrubby tree-line. He watches with amazement as his old friend and military scout, Bear Benton, steps from the bushes holding an aged and battle-scarred lever-action rifle. The buckskin-clad man with a matted, curly-gray beard, flashes a hint of a grin and shakes his head.

"Damn Holton, he already clicked off two chambers at'cha. Were you gonna wait for a hot one?"

Holton looks down at the pistol in Dull Blade's hand, as the seasoned scout scoops it away and points it skyward. Bear pulls back the hammer, squeezes the trigger and discharges a live round into the air. Holton nods and attempts to conceal his pleased surprise at seeing his old saddle-pal. "Hmm, who'd a thought you'd be in the territory?"

"Still countin' on ol' Bear to save ya I see." Bear looks down at the young injured Jules encircled by several women nursing his wounds. "Now ya got small youngun's to take yer bullets?"

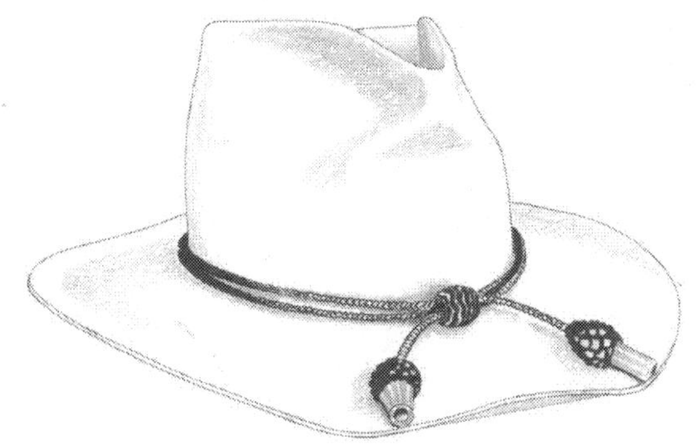

Chapter 18

Jules stares up at the grizzled military scout and eyes him curiously. Holton lowers his rifle, takes a step forward and claps his hand to Bear's shoulder. "Glad to see you old friend." The two embrace in a solid, back-slapping salutation. Bear holds Holton out at arms-length and looks him over. The older military scout notices Holton give a regretful glance down toward the dead Indian figure at his feet.

"You ain't aged nor changed at all, Holton ... some of 'em renegade redskins ain't gonna either." Holton nods and looks away from the dead bodies, while Bear studies the littered camp. He grunts a laugh and sniffs the air. "Ye still got that rangy dog?"

Bear turns as the canine crawls out from under the wagon and his guarding position by the Apache prisoners. Dog sits and peels back overhanging lips to smile his front choppers in a silent growl toward the old acquaintance. "Jeez, you really ain't changed a bit, ugly dog 'n all."

Jules continues to watch the two men converse, then finally sits up and speaks out, impatient. "Who are you, Sir?"

Bear heaves in his chest and stands at his fullest. "Who am I? Why I'm Bear Benton, the roughest, toughest Indian ..." He glances over at Holton, then back to the boy. "Uh ... *tamer* west of the Pecos and north of the Rio Bravo del Norte."

The body of Dull Blade lets out a gasp of escaped air, and Jules reaches out to kick him with his boot.

"If you tame 'em like that, you're welcome to join us." Amused, Bear turns to Holton. "He's a scrappy one ain't he?"

Holton nods and ushers Bear to follow him. After they are a few paces away from the others, Holton talks in a low voice to his old friend. "His kin was kilt in a recent raid 'n sisters taken away."

The two walk along, veering from the mess of the fight and Bear scans the several slain corpses around camp. "His sisters, huh?"

"Two of 'em were taken from a wagon train and the rest all murdered. I buried 'em where they lay, then, out of the scrub, this kid comes strolling with a regret for survivin'."

Bear halts and looks back at the ravaged campsite. "Yer leavin' a helluva path."

"How's that?"

"I come from where you left that shot dead fella at the fort and seen a Mexican corpse on yer back trail."

Holton tilts his head over toward Jules. "He's the one who done the most of it."

"Angry, huh?"

"Ain't got nothing left but thoughts of revenge."

Bear steals a glimpse at the boy, as the womenfolk finish with his remaining bandages. "What ya gonna do with him?"

Holton, with conflicted paternal feelings, watches Jules. "Figured I'd help him through and see if there is anything left on the other side."

The old friend eyes Holton curiously. "Any progress o'er on that Arizona ranch of yourn?"

"I left it as it stood."

The large, grizzly man glances back at Jules again and nods in a knowing fashion at his longtime friend's decision. He looks over the young female hostages and grimaces. "You git his sisters back?"

Holton shakes his head sadly. "Bloody Ben Sighold hauled the pair east, with another, earlier in the day 'fore we arrived."

They watch as Jules climbs to his feet, musters his strength and walks toward them. The two grown men remain quiet as Jules steps up, pauses and heaves wind into his chest to keep from blacking out. Mustering his best authority, Jules stares up at the two experienced men-of-action.

"I'm going after Bloody Ben … and Mister Lang there is going to deliver the womenfolk and prisoners to Tularosa."

Bear glances amused toward Holton. "That yer plan?"

Holton stares at Jules who is unsteady on his feet, and shakes his head slightly.

"Not exactly."

The aged military scout turns from Holton to the boy, as the young man stands and braces himself from the coming lightness in his head. Jules fights the impulse to faint and addresses Bear. "Yer welcome to ride along with me, Mister Benton, if yer up to the task."

The group stands silent as curious glances are exchanged. Bear rubs the smear-stained front of his leather fringed shirt with his palm and faces around toward Holton. "Well, I would strongly recommend yous not heading back to Fort Tularosa."

Holton glances to Jules astutely and clears his throat. "And why is that?"

Bear continues to rub his chest and scratches under his arm. "You see, there is a small, but very capable cavalry unit of US troopers that is headed this way on the trail of an escaped and accused murderer." The military scout steals a glimpse at Holton for his reaction. He looks down at Jules before continuing his story. "This certain person busted out of the guard house and made a keen enemy out of a newly, broke-nosed Sergeant."

Bear peers over accusingly at Holton, who shrugs and replies, "Things got a bit out of hand."

They both watch as Jules begins to waver on his feet. The boy looks around for support and is suddenly caught by one of the rescued girls, rushing up from behind. He reluctantly eases into her nurturing grasp, tries to catch his breath and gazes up at Bear. "Mister

Lang is innocent on all accounts. I shot that man at the fort 'fore he could flee, and I am the one who struck the soldier."

Bear smiles and appears tickled as he looks to Holton. "He do all the fighting for ya?"

"So far."

Jules nods affirmative as he looks back at the rescued hostage girl supporting him. "Do we just leave the womenfolk here for the military troopers to find and return?" She nearly drops the boy at the mention of abandonment, and Bear wags his chin to the negative.

"I wouldn't trust ol' Kilbern to do the right thing and git them gals home. He is awful bent on findin' yous both."

Holton gazes over at the group of rescued captives. "We ain't taking them further into a bigger mess of danger than they already been."

Bear scans an eye over the womenfolk as they sit and wait for the outcome of their future fate. He clears his throat and turns toward Holton. "There's a fort to the south of here a few days you are some familiar with. Maybe even a few friendly faces yet."

Jules watches Holton as the former military scout contemplates Bear's comment and replies. "Fort Davis?" Bear scratches the whiskers under his chin as he speaks thoughtfully. "Only been a year or so past."

Holton nods. "That's territory I didn't think I'd be crossing again."

Jules steadies himself back on his feet. He steps forward from the girl behind and cradles his sore arm wound. After waiting for one of the men to speak and nothing comes, he offers his suggestion. "Mister Benton can take the women to the safety of the fort, and we can continue on after my sisters."

Bear's jaw drops at the fresh proposal, looks to the young boy strangely and then says to Holton, "He's the volunteering sort, huh?"

Holton crinkles his brow at his old friend. "I know of someone else like that."

Jules turns to walk away and calls over his shoulder, "Enough of this talk! I'm riding east on my own."

After taking a few steps, the boy falters faint and is caught again by the woman alongside. Holton shoots a concerned look to his friend Bear and steps toward Jules. He stands over the injured boy and speaks sternly to him. "You'll sit in the back of the wagon for a few days 'till your wounds stop bleeding and you gain your strength."

Jules shakes the woman's grip from under his arm and turns to face Holton, his face red with ire. He looks around and spots his Walker pistol on the blanket not too far away. Marching over to it, he leans down and picks it up. Holton and Bear watch, interested, as the young boy holds the oversized horse pistol and slowly stands, wobbly in the legs and seeming light-headed.

Jules stubbornly turns to them with gun in hand, then buckles at the knees and collapses. Two of the girls rush over to him and another joins them, helping the boy to the wagon.

Holton nods affirmative and looks at Bear. "Like I said, he'll ride the wagon."

"Huh, funny kid. What was he gonna do with that loose-powder hand-cannon?"

"He's done plenty."

Bear shrugs and glances over to a tree displaying a peculiar fleshy object with a knife stuck through it. "Hey Holton, what kind o' camp you runnin' here?"

Holton looks to the shrunken male appendage fastened on the tree, then down to the dead form of Dull Blade. He shakes off the horrific image with a cringe. "Jest figured him crazier than most."

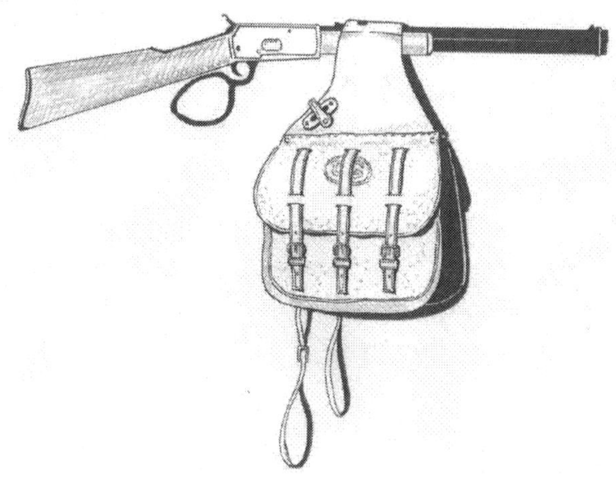

Chapter 19

The two commandeered wagons travel to the south toward Fort Davis in West Texas. Holton drives the lead wagon with the renegade Apache prisoners, while Bear follows with the other cart containing Jules and the captured women. Several saddle mounts and Indian ponies are fastened with lead ropes to the rear of the wagons, and Dog trots alongside.

Holton heaves back on the reins with a halting signal, and Bear steers his wagon alongside and stops. The burly military scout scans the open terrain and looks to Holton. "You see something?"

"Thinkin' we best make camp 'fore dark." Holton looks over his shoulder, back to their recent trail.

Bear turns to the empty landscapes behind, as well. "You worried more 'bout what could be coming behind or the memories before ya?"

"I'll have to face each of 'em in their own time."

Bear points to a tree-shaded creek running through some large rocks ahead. "O'er there, we'll at least have water." Holton nods in agreement and clucks the wagon team forward.

~*~

The evening sky over the land is clear and calm. Poncho and Gimp Ear Walt sit horseback, mounted double, about a mile distant from the wagons stopped along the small creek. They trade off watching through a brass tube spyglass, as the followed group makes camp for the night.

Gimp Ear Walt straddles the saddle cantle and looks to his partner squinting through the distance glass. The one-eared outlaw shifts uncomfortably on the warm rear flank of the sweated mount. "We gonna take them tonight?"

"You ready to get another arse-kicking already?"

"I know I'm hungry and they gots food."

"Maybe we wait 'till you git more hungry, then you don't turn tail 'n run off so fast."

In the fading light, Poncho uses the spyglass to study the camp as Walt sits quiet. The Mexican finally lowers the viewing scope, wipes his face with his hand and blinks his strained eye. "Slide off."

Walt hesitates and grips his hands to the rear saddle ties. "You ain't gonna make me walk again are ye?"

Poncho gives a sharp jab of his elbow to the body crowded behind the saddle and growls at Walt, "When I say get off, you git."

The outlaw at the rear slides backward off the horse's rump and peers up at the single rider with sad, pleading eyes. "What we gonna do, Poncho?"

Gimp Ear Walt holds the horse's tail and nervously swishes it back and forth. He holds tight, as Poncho glares down at him and speaks in his unique drawl. "We wait 'till we can take them all. Ben would no have us back empty-handed."

~*~

In the small assembled camp, the darkness of evening is beginning to descend. A central fire radiates light on the two unhitched wagons, and the women prepare a meal from the available supplies. Jules stands leaned against a wagon wheel and stares quietly into the flames. The presence of the rescued captive women only makes him more aggrieved and determined to find his own missing sisters.

At the edge of the small grouping, Holton and Bear step from the wavering firelight to talk amongst themselves. Holton looks to his old friend, as Bear taps his palm with a well-used smoking pipe, then scrapes out the charred bowl with a small stick. He watches a moment then speaks. "What's yer figure on the distance to Fort Davis?" Bear taps the empty bowl of the clay pipe on his palm again and wipes it across the chest of his fringed leather shirt.

"Another day at least." Holton steals a glance toward Jules in the camp. "That's probably about all the time I can keep that young 'un out of the saddle."

The buckskin-clad military scout takes some loose tobacco out of a pouch at his hip and begins to load the pipe. "He's like someone else I know."

The two listen quietly into the night, and Holton turns his gaze up at the dark starry sky. Bear pushes the brown malleable leaf down in the pipe and blows off the loose bits. "You know Holton, one of them women yonder has a lot of questions 'bout you."

Holton looks puzzled. "Why, what's there to say?"

Bear shrugs and smirks. He strikes a match, lets it flare and touches it to the clay pipe bowl. He takes a few puffs to light the tobacco leaf and blows out a sweet smelling smoke before answering candidly, "You did save their hides when y'all come swooping out of the wild frontier like a savior in fringed buckskin."

Holton lets his mind wander a moment, then shakes his head. "I ain't looking for a female to complicate things."

"What's there to muddle? It's jest you, the ranch and that ugly dog."

Not far away, within earshot under the wagon, Dog lets out a rumbling growl. Holton quiets him with a glance, and the animal resumes its sentinel-watch from the concealed position. "I've not been looking for companionship."

"That's usually when it comes along."

"I've been jest fine."

Bear takes a puff of the burning tobacco and, with the stem of his pipe, gestures toward Jules standing near the fire. "Gonna raise that boy by yerself when this is finished?"

"I didn't put much thought into raising him."

"Figurin' on jest droppin' him at the fort to fend for hisself like you was as a young'un?"

Holton stands quietly and thinks on the unanswered question. The familiar sounds of night chatter in the darkness, and Holton reflects on his paternal responsibility. "I ain't thought about anything but keepin' him alive."

Bear takes a short puff of the pipe and blows it out. "That's what a parent does."

Holton glances over at his perceptive friend and sees him smile in the darkness. With a hint of hostility in his voice, Holton hisses at Bear, "Why don't you raise him?"

"Sure, but only if I'm the husband 'n yer the wife."

The two men look at each other strangely, and Holton shakes off the odd proposal. "That ain't no way to talk."

The burly scout chuckles to himself and resumes his offerings of advice through occasional puffs on his clay pipe. "I'm jest tellin' you that a woman is interested in ya. Once she gets to know you, the feelin's may pass." Bear blows out a cloud of smoke that hangs in the firelight. "Or, could be she would be a good one to help the boy along with ya."

"Could be yer stickin' your nose in the sort of business that don't concern you."

Bear nods agreeably. "Could be … It happens."

The two stare out into the quiet chill of night while the fragrant aroma of tobacco smoke wafts by. The bright stars above cast shadows on the ground from the wagons and low brushy trees. Holton turns and watches, with a patriarchal fondness, as Jules takes a seat near the fire with a plate of food, and Dog slinks from under the wagon to sit near him.

Bear notices the dog's affection with interest and looks over at Holton. He finishes puffing on his pipe and wipes his gray, whiskered chin. "Oh, near forgot ta mention. Did ya see them two on the ridge when we set up camp?"

Holton nods and looks off again into the darkness. "Yeah, I figured they was the two that run off in the fight back there. One of 'em is a Mexican 'n the other is a tall skinny fella without a horse of his own."

"They gonna be trouble?"

"Eventually."

"Not tonight though?"

"They're not looking for a fair fight. They'll be along when we're at our lowest or they're at theirs."

Bear empties the used ash in the pipe and taps it on his palm. "What about Bloody Ben Sighold?"

Holton looks over at Bear and glances slightly into the campsite at Jules by the fire. "Be after him soon 'nough."

The two men exchange a look of mutual understanding as Bear utters what is on both of their minds.

"D'ya suppose that boy is 'xpectin' to find his sisters alive or the way they was before?"

Holton looks grim as the faint glow from the firelight reflects off the matured lines of his features. "Nobody will come out of this the way they was before."

Chapter 20

A small troop of US Cavalry rides through the remains of the fight in the marauder camp. Sergeant Kilbern circles his horse around and looks down at Dull Blade covered in black, crusted smears of blood. He glances over to the other Apache with his flattened head smashed to pieces.

"Bloody butchers ..." Halting his horse, Kilbern addresses his men. "These are a desperate sort of men we are after. Be extra vigilant and keep a keen eye out. We would like to capture them alive, but you are at liberty to shoot on suspicion of treachery."

The cavalry troopers circle the abandoned campsite and witness the grisly aftermath of the recent encounter. Sergeant Kilbern rides past the tree with the shriveled piece of flesh pinned to it with a knife blade. He glances at it, confused, then spurs his horse repeatedly, following the animal tracks and wagon wheel trail to the south.

~*~

The two recovered homesteader wagons travel into West Texas. The terrain opens to dusty scrubland, and Bear urges his passenger-filled wagon next to Holton's to keep out of the trailing cloud of churned wheel dust.

"Mind if I drive alongside?"

Holton looks over at Bear and grins. "Tired of choking dirt on drag?"

Bear scratches his whiskered chin and jabs a thumb over his shoulder. "Naw, them womenfolk back here have been 'a pesterin' me 'ta git a better look at ya."

The two wagons creak alongside another, and Holton glances to the cargo of female captives. He flushes with shyness, as they continually gaze over at him fondly. Holton gives the reins a slap and glares at Bear before looking forward down the trail and responding. "We should reach Fort Davis come nightfall."

The entertained military scout nods and spits a long steam of tobacco juice over the side of the wagon seat. "Yaugh, figured as much ..."

Holton's gaze travels past Bear to a rising cloud of dust created by a group of riders coming on. Bear follows Holton's stare, peers around his wagon, then speaks. "Damn Holton, our good luck might 'a jest run out. Indian's ya figure?"

"Could be."

"We gonna stand 'n fight or get gone?"

Holton squints into the far distance. "Looks to be a large party on horseback. We'd have a better chance of holding out at the fort."

"Agreed. Let's make a run for it." Bear swivels on the wooden bench seat and turns to his mostly female passengers. They eye him curiously, and the big man gives a wink toward Jules in the rear of the wagon. "Git yer heads down, hold tight 'nd don't let yer britches get bunched. We're about to go for a West Texas Dash!"

The large man takes up a fistful of reins and looks over to Holton, who levers his rifle and tucks it securely across his lap. The two exchange a knowing glance and consider the dire situation. Holton gives his old companion an affirmative nod. "You ready, Bear?"

"I was born game and plan to go out the same way!"

They both give the leather lead-lines a slap and urge on their animal team. The harness animals move forward at a lope, then stretch out to a running gallop. Sand and brush churn through the spoked wheels, as Holton and Bear race across the wide open expanse of terrain with their tethered saddle mounts running along behind.

The creaking wagons bounce and charge along, while Holton looks back at the dust cloud of faceless riders in hurried pursuit. Bear points forward to a grouping of rocks that rises up to a mountain range.

"Them's the Davis Mountains ahead. The fort should be jest beyond!"

Holton nods and slaps the reins again. The two narrow axle supply wagons seem to float behind the whirling hooves of the animal teams as the wheels spin wildly over the ground. The shrill call of a bugle catches the fleeing men's attention, and they both instantly turn to study their pursuers. Through the cloud of trailing dust, the red-over-white banner flag of the US Cavalry can be seen wavering above the column of riders.

Bear looks to Holton and keeps his wagon paced with the other. He hollers over to Holton, "I figured Kilbern only had a few troopers with 'em."

Gripping the leather lead lines, Holton shakes his head. "Well Bear, that's a whole mess more'n that!"

Holton glances at Bear and they exchange a look of trepidation. Looking down at his rifle, Holton pulls back easy on the reins and slows his heaving team of harness animals. "Easy there, whoa…" Bear slows his wagon as well and watches over his shoulder as the cavalry soldiers draw nearer. He squints to the line of troops and makes a headcount through the dusty haze.

The wagons continue along at a loping trot, going easy on the lathered animals. Bear suddenly heaves a sigh of relief and grunts loudly to his old pal, Holton. "No need to go jackrabbitin' anymore. Them's Buffalo troopers from out 'a Fort Davis."

Holton looks back over his shoulder and sees the dark, dusty riders filed in ranks, fronted by a fair-skinned officer. They ease the wagons down to a fast walk and wait for the troopers to ride up and close the gap.

The Buffalo Soldiers ride two abreast and follow along behind the swallow-tail guidon flag. The lead officer, Captain Fellows, at the head of the procession, rides up alongside Holton's wagon opposite Bear. Looking fine in his officer's uniform, the Captain leads his troopers as one of their own despite the difference in the shade of their skin.

"Hallo the wagons ..." The officer rides cautiously up next to Holton and looks down at the exposed rifle placed across his lap. His quick eye catches on the big-loop lever and he looks up, with surprise, to the man seated behind it. "Holton Lang?"

Holton looks over at the Captain and nods in agreement. A hint of recognition from his formative early years at Fort Davis shows in Holton's eyes. "Glad to see you're moving up in the world, Captain."

Bear grunts reassured as his wagon veers aside a bit. His ears perk when he hears the click of a firearm hammer being pulled back to cocked position. Bear looks behind at Jules with the Mexican carbine in hand and tucked under his arm.

After a quick glimpse around at the troopers, he gestures his hand at the youngster and whispers harshly. "Put that durned thing down, son! Them troopers are on patrol out of Fort Davis, not Tularosa. Ye cain't go shooting yer way out of every scrape ye find yerself in."

Jules keeps the rifle low and watches Holton conversing from the next wagon with the Captain. He uncocks the rifle and scoots past the womenfolk to position himself in the wooden bed just to the rear of the driver's bench. The boy talks low to Bear, as he eyes the number of troopers directly behind. "You said they had soldiers out after us."

"Yeah, but this here is a captain, not a sergeant, and them's Buffalo Soldiers under all that trail dirt."

"I ain't never seen coloreds in uniform."

"Well, if you keep on wanting to shoot everyone who comes along, you'll not see much more in yer scant years." Bear steers the wagon closer toward Captain Fellows and gives a big friendly wave toward the officer. "Good to see ya, Fellows."

The Captain drops from the procession of troopers and rides his horse around between the two moving wagons. "Why are you both back in the highlands of Texas?"

Bear gives a laugh and grumbles, "This is how it is. Holton here come into a mess of trouble and couldn't keep from gettin' me involved."

Holton responds with a slight shrug. "If there's trouble about, Bear will be along shortly."

The officer looks over to the assemblage of rescued captive women and the wound-bandaged boy in the back of Bear's wagon, then to the grim Apache prisoners in the back of Holton's. "Looks like you both have a wagon-full of mischief." The Captain tries to conceal his overwhelming curiosity and utters a logical question. "Where you coming from and where are you bound?"

Holton nods toward the north east. "A ways north of here and have to be headed that way again on the quick."

The wagon bench creaks, as Bear leans over toward the Captain and speaks in his loud blustery voice. "Ya see, we had a run in with a band of outlaws riding with Bloody Ben Sighold, and we thought it best to git these womenfolk clear 'fore following up our business with him."

Captain Fellows reins up on his mount a touch and gets a foreboding look when he hears the moniker of Bloody Ben. "I know of the wanted outlaw. Rumors are he runs mostly over to the Brazos near the Llano Estacado."

Bear offer an amenable shrug and continues, "Well, he murdered several groups of homesteaders, took these womenfolk as captives and teamed up with them renegade Apache ya see there. We figured we could deliver 'em all to you boys in blue."

The Captain rides along quiet as the procession continues, and the cavalry man contemplates their options. Finally, he looks back at his following troopers and addresses Holton and Bear in the wagons. "They run a stage line through on the lower road from San Antonio that we've been patrolling. Guess we can hold 'em at the fort 'ntil we can find a place for 'em."

Holton glances over at the Captain and inquires, guardedly, "Merritt still in command at the fort?"

As Fellows nods, Bear guffaws, "How is Ol' Stone Britches?"

"He is on his way out. We have another coming in by the name of Hatch that should be arriving within the week."

The wagons and troops continue to travel along toward the fort location at the base of the mountain range, and Holton looks over to Jules with the Sharps rifle still in hand. He turns to Captain Fellows riding alongside. "We've got other business to attend, so if you boys could escort these wagons and cargo into Fort Davis, we'd be much obliged and can be on our way."

The officer turns his head and scans around at the wagon's occupants, then his column of road-weary troopers. "Be glad to escort you to the fort and help you unload your burden. I will have to insist that you report a detailed account with the commanding officer."

Bear looks over at Holton, and they silently weigh their options. The seasoned military scout recognizes their lack of choices, nods to Holton and grimaces, as he spits over the side of the turning wheel. "Well Captain, if you insist."

The cavalry officer turns from Holton to Bear and salutes. "Very well then, I will escort you and Mister Lang onto the grounds at Fort Davis."

Holton rests his hands across the big-loop rifle on his lap. "Lead the way, Captain ..." Captain Fellows rides ahead and waves the ranks of dusty horse soldiers onward.

As the captain clears the position between the two wagons, Bear exchanges an apprehensive look with Holton. Bear looks behind at Jules and slaps his leather reins, urging the harness team after the column of cavalry.

"Sit back, kid. We're on to Fort Davis."

Jules hangs from the wooden backrest of the driver's bench and watches the Buffalo Soldiers file past. "What about them following us from the north?"

Bear peers behind, through the rolled up sides of the canvas wagon cover, to the empty horizon on their back trail. "Hopefully we get clear of the fort yonder before they arrive, or things might get a mite complicated..." The grizzled scout slaps leather lines and the team steps up to the quickened pace of the other wagon and mounted troopers. In the distance, the familiar adobe structures of Fort Davis can be made out on the landscape, backed by the dark mountains of rock reaching up toward the sky.

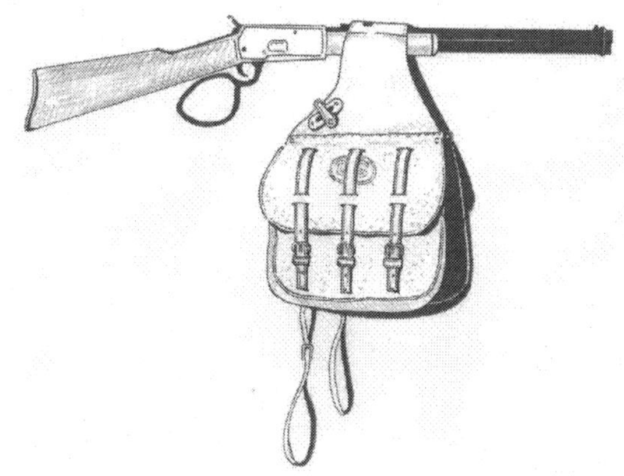

Chapter 21

The troops of Buffalo Soldiers lead Holton and Bear's wagons across the military fort parade grounds. The column halts near the commissary building and Captain Fellows rides over and pulls up his mount next to Holton's wagon. "I will be making a report to Lieutenant Colonel Merritt promptly and will inform him of your situation. He will more than likely want to talk with you on the morrow."

Bear tosses the reins aside and hops from the wagon. "Let's go see the old Indian-rustler right now!"

Holton wraps the leather harness lines around the brake handle and looks to Jules in the wagon ahead of him, seated with the women. The boy holds the Sharps rifle and starts to climb down. Their gazes meet, and Holton calls out to the boy, "I want you to stay with the wagons."

Captain Fellows relieves command of his troopers to a sergeant who leads them away toward the barracks. The officer watches them file past and looks to Bear, then Holton.

"You both may accompany me to Merritt's quarters and, possibly, he will talk with you tonight."

Holton steps down from the wagon bench next to the horseback captain. "That would be best." With his big-loop rifle in hand, Holton looks over and gives Dog an indicating gesture toward Jules.

The rangy canine sits, attentive, near the wagon, as the boy stands in the cargo-filled bed. Jules holds the rifle at his side as he looks down at Dog, then watches Holton and Bear follow the Captain.

~*~

The afternoon sun dips low behind the horizon as Holton and Bear stand outside Lt. Col. Wesley Merritt's quarters waiting to be invited in. Bear tongues the tobacco chaw in his cheek and whispers loudly, "Ya'd think the old Indian fighter would see us right off, after what we done for him in the past!"

"Who knows what's on his plate."

With a huff, Bear tries to peek through a wavy glass window pane. "Good army beef most likely…" Bear gazes around and spits off to the side before continuing. "I do know we don't want to hang around this military outpost for long. That bent-on-revenge sergeant from up north was sent out with a patrol to find you and bring you in."

Holton watches the recovered materials from the wagons being unloaded across the parade grounds. A hint of a smile appears as he glimpses over at Bear. "Maybe he's given it up by now."

Bear looks to Holton doubtfully and shakes his head to the negative. "Naw, he's got a real good dose of busted pride along with that squashed nose of his."

"We'll talk with Merritt first and get clear tonight."

"Sooner the better."

~*~

The office anteroom door opens and Captain Fellows stands looking out at Bear and Holton. He steps aside and ushers them in. Holton holds his rifle in hand as he crosses the threshold, and Bear hooks his finger into his cheek to toss away the juicy wad of chaw before entering.

Holton and Bear follow Captain Fellows into Merritt's office and see the commander seated behind his desk. He has his military blouse pulled on and half buttoned up the chest. The quarters are in piled disarray from being in the midst of organization and packing.

The Lieutenant Colonel looks the part of a seasoned veteran of the Indian Wars with his silver streaked moustache and keen, sun-squinted eyes. Although seemingly half-dressed without his head covering, he appears distinguished in his uniform and is an inspiration and fine example to the enlisted men who follow him. Merritt watches the men enter, then stands and salutes. "Hello to the pair of you. Bear, I heard you were off fighting Indians in Arizona."

Bear scuffs his boot toe on the plank floor, smiles and settles into an old familiar rapport with Merritt.

"Too damned hot! Moved north into Nuevo Mexico to chase the sort of Apache I'm more familiar with. Them rascals jump the reservation regular, and I'm on their trail to bring 'em back or chase 'em south."

Merritt sniffs as his moustache twitches, and he turns his steely gaze to Holton. "Holton Lang … you left a mighty big boot-print 'round these parts of Texas. The tales have gotten so tall that I doubt even you will measure up to them."

Holton tilts his head toward his companion alongside. "No thanks to Bear here, I assume."

Bear puffs out his chest a bit. "Well, I cain't jest be talkin' 'bout myself all the time."

The Lieutenant Colonel looks down at the special big-loop rifle at Holton's side. "That prize rifle has become the biggest celebrity in Texas since Crockett's Ol' Betsy."

Holton looks down at the well-used gun and shrugs. "It's just a good workin' gun, no better or worse than the man who uses it."

Merritt settles back into his chair and peers up at the buckskin-clad pair of former scouts. "So, Captain Fellows informs me you took a wagon of goods and female captives from Bloody Ben Sighold?"

Bear steps forward and offers up his unsolicited opinion on the matter. "Holton practically done it all on his own with another. I just happened along to help him deliver them here."

The military officer grins, amused. "As always, Bear, you are too modest."

"I've been accused of worse."

Holton clears his throat and speaks. "We would like to leave them here in your care and continue on."

Merritt sits behind his desk and ponders thoughtfully a moment. He looks at Bear, then Holton. "You may have heard, I'm on my way out from my duties here at Fort Davis. Haven't been officially reassigned, but the new feller, Hatch is due here in the next few days."

Bear sniffs and grunts, "Good luck to ya then."

"I would entreat that you both stick around until the new Commanding Officer arrives. I know you won't heed my request, so I'll have to require it."

Holton glances at Bear, then turns to Merritt.

"Sir, we have business to the north."

"Bloody Ben Sighold?"

Holton nods to the seated officer. "He trailed east with several more hostages 'fore we encountered the rest."

Merritt stares down at the papers on his desk then turns to the darkening, sun-glinted window. "Turning over this command is difficult enough. I would rather not have any loose ends."

Holton clenches his jaw and speaks direct. "We come here voluntary and will leave the same."

Merritt continues to look outside and murmurs aloud. "It should only be a day or two."

Bear stands erect and puts up his best salute. "Yes, Sir! Be glad to stick around."

Holton looks to Captain Fellows standing behind them and shoots Bear a quizzical glance. The burly scout drops his salute, scratches his beard and ushers Holton to the door. Merritt watches them keenly and half stands as he calls out, "Now, I mean it Bear."

"You bettcha, you know me." Bear shoves Holton through the doorway and quickly pulls it closed behind him.

Captain Fellows steps to the desk from beside the doorway and stands at attention. Merritt rises and pushes his chair back to address the officer. "Captain, get a statement from each of the recovered captives that those two brought in. Put Bear and Mister Lang under lock and key, if necessary, to keep them here, but I want this wrapped up nicely when Hatch arrives."

Fellows nods with acceptance of his orders and speaks. "What of the Apache they brought in?"

"Get their statements, if any are to be had, and we'll let the new commander dish out their sentence."

Merritt snaps off a salute, and Captain Fellows returns the gesture before exiting the room. The Lieutenant Colonel turns around to study the wall map of the West Texas frontier. He reminisces on long-past expeditions and conflicts engaged to defend the pioneer settlements from the warring Apache. The uniformed military man gazes reflectively into the sketched lines of detailed terrain, pondering quietly, as if saying a silent goodbye.

Chapter 22

Holton and Bear walk to the wagons near the commissary. The lights from inside the other post buildings cast long shadows from the wagons across their path. Bear leans over and whispers as they walk. "Holton, we have to play this careful."

A firm look comes over Holton's features, as he glances past his shoulder for anyone listening before responding. "I'm not sticking around for a few days just to tell war stories to another uniform."

"Didn't figure you would, and if Sergeant Kilbern arrives from Fort Tularosa while yer here, you ain't going away anytime too quick."

The quiet crunch of gravel is heard as the two men step up to the empty wagons. They both seem to sense a presence watching from the darkness. They pause until one of the captive women steps from the shadows near Holton.

"Mister Lang, I have to tell you something..."

Holton is disconcerted by the shaky fear in the young woman's voice. He turns to Bear, and the scout quickly ushers them both to concealment behind the wagon.

Bear dims a nearby lantern and addresses the female with a loud whisper. "What is it, girl?"

A small shaft of light from the nearby commissary shines on the girl's anxious features. "The boy... he and Alice took two of the saddled Indian ponies and headed north after the other stolen ones."

Holton leans in close to the nervous girl and watches her shadowed expression earnestly. "When did they leave?"

"About an hour ago."

Bear puts his hand to Holton's shoulder and talks low. "Ya gonna go after them in the dark?"

Holton gives a low signaling whistle and gets no response from Dog. The young woman watches Holton listening into the darkness and offers a timid explanation. "That wild dog ain't around. He followed them both on their heels like he was shepherding them. They told the guard they left something off the wagon outside the fort and needed to fetch it. They went out and didn't come back."

The usual sounds of the fort surroundings are mostly quiet as Bear peeks around the wagon and looks toward the front gate. Two men stand guard alongside the heavy, wooden-arched doors. "They ain't gonna jest let you out to go lookin' for 'em."

Holton's features are stern with determination. "They'll have a hard time of it stoppin' me."

An electric sort of energy zips through the air as the sound of shuffling feet on gravel draws near. Several uniform clad troopers step around the empty wagon and hold their carbines firmly across their chests. Captain Fellows appears from behind the soldiers and looks to Holton and Bear with the woman. He studies the three a moment and senses Holton's purpose on departure. "Mister Lang, I am afraid we must insist you stay on."

Bear looks at the perceptive captain and his armed escort of ready troopers. He turns up the flame on the nearby oil lamp and lets out a dejected sigh. Holton points his gaze over to the front gates and finally back to the Captain with a slight nod.

~*~

The complete darkness of night is all-consuming, with heavy clouds covering the stars and a slim crescent moon. Mounted on two Indian ponies, Jules and the woman, Alice, ride quietly north. The silence around them is broken only by the crunching of brush and rock beneath unshod hooves.

The fair-haired female riding alongside Jules hides her lean and womanly figure beneath a pair of men's trousers and an old, drop-sleeve shirt. Alice Weathersby adjusts her pulled-up hair under a floppy brimmed hat and rests Jules' acquired Mexican rifle over her lap as she rides. A birdcall whistles out into the night, and Jules looks to Alice in the darkness.

The boy slows his horse next to hers and for the first time, there is a hint of unsteadiness in his voice. "Maybe this wasn't a good idea… leaving at night?"

"They wouldn't have let us go otherwise."

Jules pauses and listens for the unusual bird call again. "Holton has been good to me and said he would help."

"He seems to be a good man."

Uncertain, Jules peers back in the direction of the fort. "Maybe we should turn around and wait for him."

Alice shakes her head, and Jules tries to make out her features in the dark shadows under the floppy hat. Her face remains obscured as she speaks and urges her mount forward. "Those soldiers won't do anything but stick you on a coach headed for an orphanage in San Antonio and send me back somewhere east to a family that doesn't exist."

Jules looks down at the Walker pistol nested on his lap. "I reckon yer right. I'll jest have to kill Bloody Ben myself if I want to get my sisters back."

The boy and woman continue riding along the dark midnight trail, and the clouds above break momentarily. On the path ahead, silhouetted in the darkness, they spot the figure of a man standing next to a saddled horse. As they step closer, Alice grips the short rifle and calls out in warning, "Who's there?"

Jules raises his large pistol and pulls back the hammer with a heavy click. Suddenly a dark figure dashes from the night, grabs a hold of the boy's arm and jerks the Walker pistol away. Alice tries to pull back the hammer on the Sharps rifle, and it slips from her grasp and clanks to the ground at her horse's feet. She considers jumping down to retrieve the gun but instead remains astride her mount next to Jules, as they both wait silently.

They hear the clinking sound of large, heavy roweled spurs dragging on the ground, as the man walks toward them. He picks up the rifle on the trail and looks up at the two young faces in the dark. The man reaches into a vest pocket, and the scrape of a match against a fingernail sputters and flickers a flame. Poncho Ruiz lights a small cigar held between his teeth and takes a puff. "You look for Ben Sighold, eh? We take you to 'im..."

Like a demon, he blows exhaled smoke through flared nostrils. In a clouded haze, the Mexican man extinguishes the flaming matchstick, and they are all left as silhouettes in the scant moonlight.

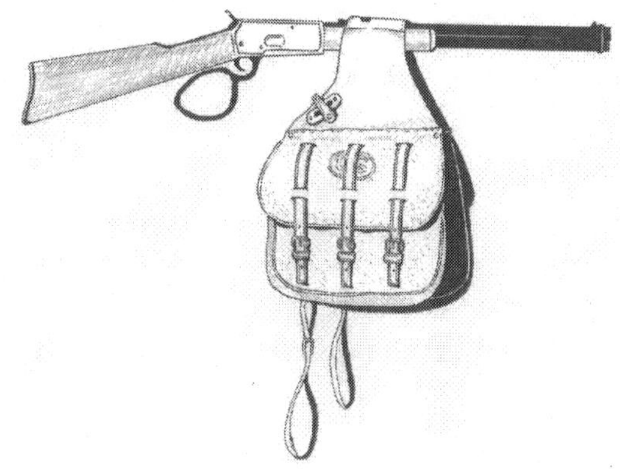

Chapter 23

Holton paces the floor of the isolated barrack as the morning sun comes in through the glass-paned window. He stares out to the early light while Bear lies on a military cot and pretends to sleep.

The burly scout rolls over and opens an inquisitive eye. "Any ideas yet?"

"Depends. Are you coming along?"

"I sure don't fancy sticking 'round here 'nd answering all the silly questions about you and what you were thinking 'fore you took yer leave."

The former resident of the fort stops at the window and stares out to the familiar environs of the military compound. Holton thinks back to what seems to be a lifetime ago, when he was young and once called this soldierly establishment home. His age would have been about that of Jules when he was orphaned to the hospitality of the military post.

Holton speaks over his shoulder towards Bear. "We will need to have our horses saddled outside the fort walls and ready. I don't want to have to charge the gate and get anyone hurt."

Bear lounges back on the stiff bunk and scratches the whiskers around his neck. "I could maybe get one of them gals to do it. Should be able to work it out when we take the morning meal."

Holton nods and continues to stare at the gate outside. "That's fine. Any of them you can trust to keep their movements quiet and above suspicion?"

The burly scout smiles, closes his eyes and puts his hands up behind his head. "Well, the one who fancied you went off with the boy."

A puzzled look crosses Holton's countenance, and he turns to look at Bear, who continues to lay back and rest. Holton watches his old friend attempt to sleep and probes for some sort of reasoning for her actions. "Why'd she do that?"

Bear groans and sits up on the military cot. "You asking me why a woman does something?"

Holton shakes his head in wonderment. "It don't make sense them going off."

The cot creaks under the shifting of weight and Bear scratches under his bearded chin again. He squints a half-opened eye toward Holton and clears his throat. "From what I learned as their temporary chaperone …" Bear notices Holton's attentive interest as he speaks. "That gal, Alice, was taken from a ranch, somewheres up north. Her family was all killed, including a husband

and two boys. It don't make no sense not to want some kind of revenge, 'n ta kill the ones who done it."

Holton looks to his hat and rifle propped up near a neatly made bed that hasn't been slept in. "We ain't under guard, so if we can get our saddled mounts out of these walls and waiting, we kin slip out."

The sound of a commotion at the front gate catches his attention, and Holton moves to the window again. The two main gates are swung open wide and Sergeant Kilbern rides in, followed by US Cavalry troopers. Holton strides across the room and grabs up his hat and rifle. He glances aside to Bear and murmurs, "Things jest got complicated."

Bear jumps to his feet and looks out the window as the guard at the gate gestures in their general vicinity. The roused, older military scout ducks away from the barracks window and grunts, "Damn!" Bear jams his hat down on his head and peeks outside again. "Yep, they're lookin' this way."

Holton grabs up his saddle bags and moves to the door with Bear close on his heels. Before they step outside, the burly scout puts his hand to his friend's shoulder and half turns him around. "Where ya goin'?"

"I'm leaving."

"How? Ya cain't."

"I've done it before."

"Yeah, but hell … this seems a mite different."

The two buckskin-clad former scouts step outside the barracks building and scan the garrison. The attention from Kilbern's entrance has gathered everyone within earshot of the front gates. Bear watches, as Holton crosses the parade grounds on foot in a direct path to the horse corrals.

Halfway across the wide open area, Sergeant Kilbern recognizes the tall lean figure of Holton Lang and maneuvers his horse away from the assembled crowd. Without a call of warning, Kilbern puts his horse to a lope then spurs hard to a running gallop, charging at Holton across the wide empty space between.

The sound of the running animal turns Holton, and he faces off with the sergeant. Their eyes lock across the distance and Holton quickly realizes Kilbern's intentions of running him down without mercy. Rifle in hand, Holton hesitantly glances down at the gun and makes a split-second decision. He drops his saddle bags from his shoulder and breaks into a run toward the charging force of man astride beast.

The two figures close the expanse of ground, running full tilt; man afoot in direct challenge to another charging on horseback. The seconds hang in the air as the two come together. At the final moment before a head-on collision, the horse shies from its course and shimmies to the side.

Holton takes a running leap and smashes into the mounted torso of Sergeant Kilbern. The two men tumble back over the squatted flank of the horse, as the saddle animal stumbles and falls away. The buckskin-clad westerner is quickly over top the uniformed sergeant. Using his grip on the rifle, Holton smashes the big-loop lever like a set of steel knuckles across the military man's jaw.

The two climb to their feet in the middle of the parade grounds and face off. Holton drops his rifle to the side and the two men lunge forcefully at each other. Fist whirling over fist, the men exchange hammered blows that crack and echo from the open air bout.

Both men give as good as they get, and the two fighters duke it out, seemingly equally matched. The scuffle is quickly encircled by an assemblage of inquisitive fort personnel and Buffalo Soldiers. The crowd begins to place bets, while they cheer and applaud the swinging combatants.

Holton delivers another teeth-rattling blow to Kilbern, and the sergeant stumbles back and flops in the dirt. One of the white soldiers from Fort Tularosa, with his carbine in hand, steps from the mostly dark-skinned crowd. "Holton Lang, you're under arrest!"

As Holton turns to face the trooper, the man swings his rifle across Holton's temple and knocks him to the ground. His head pounding in a daze, Holton looks up at the attacking soldier as the man raises his rifle to strike another crushing blow. A flash of blue uniform emerges from the crowd of onlookers, and a Buffalo Soldier reaches out with an embracing tackle of the man with the rifle. Several of the other fair-skinned troopers from Fort Tularosa step into the foray and are quickly swept into a fist-flying brawl with the surrounding troops of Fort Davis.

Holton climbs to his feet during the melee and looks toward Sergeant Kilbern as he tries to prop himself up on an elbow. Suddenly a military bugle call pierces the air and the scuffle slowly loses its punch. The authoritative presence of Lieutenant Colonel Merritt steps into the crowd and the disheveled troopers stand at attention. "What is the meaning of this fracas?"

Sergeant Kilbern is helped to his feet by two of his men and stands with his face a blood-smeared mess. He tries to rise himself to attention as he stands before Merritt. "My prisoner was resisting arrest, Sir."

Merritt follows Kilbern's weak gesture toward Holton, and he looks over the former scout, tilting his head questioningly. "Prisoner?"

Kilbern spits blood from his mouth and glares at Holton. "He escaped from Fort Tularosa a few days ago and is wanted for murder."

The stoic commanding officer stands rigid before Sergeant Kilbern, studies him a moment, then looks again to Holton. "Is what he says true?"

"That's his version of it."

Merritt takes a deep calming breath and looks around at the scuffle-weary soldiers presented before him. "A sort of misunderstanding, I presume?"

Holton nods and Kilbern steps forward. "I'm taking him back with me to Fort Tularosa."

Merritt turns to the lower ranked individual and stares him down with a gaze of experienced authority. "You'll do nothing of the kind until I say so." The Lieutenant Colonel turns to the military officer beside him and musters up the unchallenged tone of his rank. "Captain! Put every man involved in this juvenile mess under house arrest."

Merritt looks across at Bear, still holding one of the troopers from Fort Tularosa on the ground under his boot heel. "Bear, you involved with this?"

"No, Sir."

"Please escort Mister Lang back to his quarters and keep him there until I unravel the cause of this situation."

Merritt turns to Kilbern as the sergeant wavers before him. "Sergeant, get yourself cleaned up and report to my quarters within the hour." The commanding officer takes one last look at Holton, shakes his head reproachfully and marches out of the crowd.

Bear looks down at the restrained trooper underfoot and smiles as he lifts his hat in a salutation. He removes his boot from the man's chest, and the trooper heaves a lungful of air. Bear walks over and lifts the big-loop rifle from the ground and he gives an inviting wave toward Holton. "C'mon, ya old pig wrestler. Looks like yer in it again."

Holton watches the short procession of tousled soldiers who were involved in the scrap as they are ushered in step, marching across the parade grounds under military arrest. One of the dark-skinned troopers looks to Holton and gives a smile and salute. Holton nods with gratitude as he watches them file away. He touches his bleeding lip with his tongue and flexes his bloodied knuckles before turning to Bear.

"What now?"

"Well, you ain't goin' after that kid anytime soon."

Bear slaps Holton on the back, causing a cloud of dry dirt and dead grass to flutter off. He looks at his longtime friend and shakes his head, unsurprised at the complicated situation. Bear ushers him forward, then walks alongside him back to the barracks.

Chapter 24

A sentry stands outside the military barracks at the entrance door to where Holton and Bear are being detained. Inside, Bear lounges on a cot with the big-loop rifle nearby, as Holton watches out the window. His boot heels kicked up on the adobe wall, Bear turns his head toward Holton.

"We ain't got much further than we were this morning. 'Cept now you have a busted lip."

Holton peers over at Bear and flexes his sore shoulder. "I ain't sticking 'round here long."

The thick-chested, bearded scout on the cot heaves a deep breath and adjusts his booted feet on the gritty dirt wall. "Look on the bright side … Merritt must like ya some still. If he didn't, he'd have you in the brig."

Holton stands at the window until there is a soft knock. Both men turn and watch as the door slowly opens and a soldier enters. The colored trooper holds himself proudly and looks over to Holton with a mysterious look of admiration.

"Hello, Sirs. I was appointed to watch over you's both till my orders are told different."

Grit falls from the wall as Bear repositions his feet with a grunt. "How 'bout something to eat?"

The trooper stands at the door a long moment and smiles a shy grin. Bear and Holton watch him awhile then look to each other curiously.

Bear is the first to speak up. "What? Did I miss something funny?"

The Buffalo Soldier continues to grin a clear white smile, and his eyes dart to the floor bashfully. "You's both probably don't remember me from the shootin' contest, here at the fort, a long while back."

Holton smiles as the private glances to the special big-loop rifle. "Private Dedman?"

"Yes, Sir."

"Hah, glad to see you again."

Moving away from the window, Holton steps up to Private Dedman and extends his open hand for a handshake. "Heck soldier … seems a lifetime ago."

Dedman reaches out and gladly grasps Holton's hand. "Yes, Sir. Glad to be in the esteemed company of Mister Holton Lang again myself." The uniformed private gives Holton a firm handshake and looks to Bear lounging on the army cot. He stands straight and gives the military scout a smart salute. "The stories told by Bear Benton are legendary 'round these parts of Texas."

Bear grins and looks to Dedman with interest. "Dedman, huh?" The burly man kicks his feet off the wall and swings around to a sitting position with his boots on the floor. "Yeah, I remember you. Any news of that youngun' scout, Denny Spreene?"

"Yes, Sir. Last time I heard, he'd taken up a ranch few days east of here near Fort Clark."

"Hmm, too bad... I could've used his help 'bout now."

Private Dedman takes a quick glimpse over his shoulder, as he steps inside and closes the door behind him. "Maybe yous need to get out from here and continue yer urgent business north?"

Holton looks over at Bear, who appears pleasantly shocked. The large scout rises to his feet and steps closer as he speaks. "Well, maybe we do."

Holton glances out the window at the small grouping of guarding soldiers outside and back at Dedman. "What did you have in mind?

Dedman beams at Holton then turns to Bear.

"Ya see ... the Colonel is in a bit of a tight spot here. He can't officially let you go to yer business, but he feels he owes you some of a debt for your past service."

Bear gives a huff and nudges Holton.

"He probably jest don't want to deal with the colossal mess been made here since you arrived. Best thing to do is git you and that resentful sergeant as far away as possible."

The private stands straight at attention and salutes. "Yes Sir. Colonel says to get them two ex-dispatch riders out of this fort and clear of the new command 'fore they turn the whole place into a barroom brawl." After Dedman relays his message to the two recent detainees, he stands at rest.

Bear smiles proudly. "He's lettin' us go?"

The private shakes his head negative and talks low. "No, Sir… not exactly. But he *is* letting me unofficially escort you wherever you need to git, as long as it happens 'fore the new commanding officer arrives."

Bear, wrapping his arm around Private Dedman's shoulder, says, "The sooner, the better."

"That's what the Colonel says too."

Crossing the room to take up his rifle and hat, Holton peers out the window before he turns to the Buffalo Soldier. "We're ready when you are."

Bear thumps Dedman's woolen jacket and looks him over with an approving nod. The soldier puts his hand on the door handle and speaks quiet. "Everything should be ready within the hour."

With a snort, Bear goes to gather his things then turns back to the soldier. "How 'bout some grub?"

Dedman smiles slyly as he watches the two men.

"Yes, Sir. You's be gettin' plenty of that."

Bear and Holton both look to the wide-grinning trooper and are oddly intrigued.

~*~

Four riders on three horses travel north toward the Llano Estacado. The Mexican bandit, Poncho leads the group with Jules and Alice following behind, riding double. Gimp Ear Walt brings up the rear astride one of the recaptured Indian ponies. The one-eared bandit holds the boy's Sharps rifle and anxiously glances around at the hilly surroundings.

Seated in the saddle, Jules gives a reassuring look to Alice as she holds on to him behind the cantle. He slows their walking pace to ride alongside Walt and asks, "Why are you so nervous, mister?"

"Who says?"

"You do."

Walt looks to the woman then the boy curiously and grunts, "I ain't said squat."

"All your lookin' back regular says plenty."

Gimp Ear Walt stares at the kid and woman horseback alongside and whispers, "What happened with all them Injuns from the camp?"

"Some are dead and the others taken prisoner."

"All of 'em?"

Now seeming to understanding the paranoid fears of the bandit, Jules can't help but grin. "Most of them … 'cept the craziest one."

Walt glances over his shoulder and watches their trail. "What about that other feller you was riding with?"

The amused smile drops from the boy's features, and he looks behind past Alice seated on the horse's hindquarters. "He ain't interested in what I have to do."

"Why's that?"

"There's nothing in it for him."

Walt nods, satisfied with the boy's simple reasoning. They ride along awhile, and Jules continues his probing. "How far are we going?"

"Till we get there."

"Texas?"

Walt shrugs as if afraid to say too much. "Maybe ... It will be all the same to you."

"You gonna show up empty-handed?"

The one-eared man nervously looks ahead at Poncho, riding in the lead and back at Jules. "Ben will be plenty glad to git his hands on the little shit-fire who shot 'em in the mouth."

"What's he going to do … kill me?"

Smiling, Walt rubs the stub of an ear on his head and laughs as he thinks aloud, "Bloody Ben's funny 'bout things. He'll probably shoot you in the mouth for starters to even things up, then he'll maybe cut at ya a bit to account for all the trouble you've made for him."

Jules puts on a brave face, as he peers over his shoulder at Alice riding behind. He nudges his horse alongside Walt and speaks softly to the man's good ear. "Don't ya think he'll be some upset with you for losing everything worth any profit in them wagons?"

Walt looks sidelong at Jules and crinkles his forehead. "You pushing at me, boy?"

"Just thought you might want to think about it."

"What 'bout that girl we got?"

"She's old compared to the ones you left behind."

Alice peers over Jules' shoulder and listens attentively to the boy trying to prod and irritate the outlaw. The one-eared bandit can't help thinking of Bloody Ben's reputation. Thoughts of the impending wrath give Walt a fearful shiver. "Well, she's all we got."

"Could be you should rob a bank or something more profitable on the way."

Ahead, Poncho deliberately slows his horse and waits for the others to move up next to him. He turns in the saddle toward Jules and Alice then stares coldly at the boy.

"Could be I should cut out your young, wiggly tongue and feed it to that mangy dog that follows."

Jules looks behind down the trail and sees Dog pause and sit about fifty yards away. Poncho reaches over, grabs the stud decorated Sharps rifle from Walt's hands and pulls back the hammer to cocked positon.

The Mexican takes careful aim at the canine and Jules pushes the barrel aside just as he pulls the trigger. The shot goes off target and smashes into the nearby brush. Poncho glares fiercely at Jules and holds his hand out to Walt for another loaded cartridge. Gimp Eared Walt finds another long, brass rifle round in the saddlebag and holds it out to the angered Mexican.

Poncho levers the breach, tosses away the empty brass shell casing and loads the fresh round. He gives a warning stare toward Jules and raises the rifle to his shoulder again. As the squint-eyed bandit draws a lethal bead on Dog, the canine suddenly darts away into the underbrush.

Poncho lets out an impatient sigh and lowers his aim. He uncocks the hammer and angrily tosses the rifle back to Gimp Ear Walt. Jules smiles, relieved, and the Mexican pulls his bone-handled skinning knife from its sheath.

In a flash, Poncho reaches out and grabs Alice by the hair at the back of her head and pulls her close. He sends a cold stare toward Jules as he lets the sharp knife glimmer in the midday sunlight. "You are a little boy that is much trouble. I hear you talk trouble again and I will cut off her lips." Poncho holds the knife blade under Alice's quivering mouth and applies slight pressure.

"Have you seen a woman without lips? They have a smile to them that is all teeth … all the time." He pushes Alice away to her position behind the saddle cantle and sheathes his knife. Poncho stares at Jules with an icy glare, puts a finger to his lips, then smiles with menace. "Shhh, hijo …"

Jules turns to Alice, seated behind him in trembling shock, and observes the raw fear in the woman's eyes. He quietly nods toward Poncho, and the Mexican smiles, satisfied. "Good, let's go. We have another two days ride to the canyons along the Brazos."

Chapter 25

Several apron-clad troopers haul buckets and crates of mess hall trash to a wooden military escort wagon. Another soldier steps up to the driver's box and takes hold of the reins. Turning the harness team, he drives across the parade grounds and stops the wagon in front of Private Dedman, who waits at the door to one of the barracks buildings.

The trooper driving the wagon steps down, giving a casual salute, and walks back toward the mess hall. Bear and Holton stand in the shadows behind

Dedman, and the smell of rotting food and kitchen garbage is strong in the air. Bear snorts disgruntled out his nostrils and wipes his lip whiskers. "When I asked about some grub, I had something completely different in mind."

The foul smell of the wagon doesn't seem to irritate the horses as they wait patiently with their heads lowered. Private Dedman looks over his shoulder and grins. "Turns out, this is the best way to get yous both out of the fort and not cause any trouble. We have your gear and horses saddled about a mile down the trail."

The dark-skinned soldier moves around behind the wagon and drops the wooden tailgate to reveal the empty bed under a false upper decking that holds the rubbish. Dedman gives a welcoming salute and near whispers, "All aboard."

Holton steps forward and hands his big-loop rifle to Dedman. He removes his hat, glances around and slides into the concealed space. With a groan, Bear pulls his beat-up felt hat down on his head and crawls inside next to Holton. The big man shimmies along the wood slab bottom and mumbles, "I ain't done something like this since I was huntin' buffalo near the Palo Pinto. I had to hide in one of them puffed up carcasses to keep out of sight from the Comanche."

Holton gives an exaggerated, examining sniff, as Bear slides in next to him in the cramped cavity. "I bet it smelled a mite better'n this too."

"Hrmph … me or the rubbish?"

"Cain't hardly tell the difference."

Holton tries to stifle a chuckling laugh, as Bear wiggles around to get situated. He jabs his elbow into Holton's ribs and in the dimness of the wagon nook, Bear turns to face his pal. "If I could move any more, I'd sock ya right in the jaw."

"Do it on my right as my left is still a touch sore."

The light goes out of the wood-slat hollow, as Private Dedman lifts and fastens the heavy tailgate closed. "Hush now you two. Only a few select folks knows 'bout yous headed out this way. Cause me a lot of trouble to explain a talkin' wagon box full 'a slop."

The space beneath the wagon's load is muted and almost completely dark, as they listen to Dedman walk around and climb up into the driver's box. The two inside wait and take note of the other's stifled breath until the wagon jerks forward and creaks along on greased axles. Small cracks of white light beam in through the slits in the sideboard slats, and small bits of food-trash particles fall through the gaps in the covering boards above.

Bear spits aside and tries to reach his hand up to wipe the scrap bits from his beard. "Sphewwy … that grub up there is more'n a week old."

Holton chokes back a laugh and turns his head to keep the rubbish from landing on his face. He slides his hat over as a shield and watches as Bear scrunches his eyes and mouth.

The wagon reaches the front gate, and the two can hear the hushed voices outside converse. The words sound distant and unintelligible through the thick sideboards and load of mess hall trash. Finally the wagon lunges forward again and travels out of Fort Davis on the faint trail to the north.

~*~

Isolated on the cap rock above the canyons formed by the Brazos River, a horseback rider leads three females, with their hands bound, atop Indian ponies. Bloody Ben Sighold looks back at his hostages as they slump over the necks of the trailing mounts.

He barks irritably back at them as they stare ahead, tired and weary. "Sit up and look alive! We are almost there and my Comanchero friends don't like weak crying babies." One of the girls sits up slightly and grits her teeth and the pair of younger ones continues to sniffle and slouch.

A sharp wail of advancing voices shocks the girls into silence, and they look around frightfully. Bloody Ben holds his open hand high and waves to the dozen riders, as they rise out of the canyons from the watershed below. The mounted riders are a mix of Comanche natives and white outlaws who look even harder than the previous band of men Bloody Ben was associated with.

As the riders near, Ben eases the pistol from his holster and lays it across his lap. His sharp gaze studies the gathering of men suspiciously. "Hail, Black Hand … I bring you and your men gifts."

The leader of the horseback assembly slide-stops his mount in front of Ben and stares past him to the hostage women. The Comanche, Black Hand, is a tall sturdy warrior who has fought many years against the onslaught of settlers and military, and has steered clear of the reservation lands they have tried to keep him on. With his band of hostile warriors and outlaws hidden away in the canyons of northern Texas, he raids and pillages as he pleases. The most significant marking on the tall Comanche leader is the image of an open hand pressed across his chest in a dark, cracked paint, the consistency of dried blood.

Black Hand's intimidating stare returns back to Bloody Ben after his attentive considerations of the hostage women. He smiles wickedly when he notices the scabbed-over, ragged scar on the white man's whisker-stubble cheek. "You catch bullet in teeth?"

Ben scowls as the outlaws and savages encircle his prisoners. In a primitive Comanche dialect, Bloody Ben Sighold responds to Black Hand's taunt. "I catch bullets in many places, but don't ever die."

The Comanche grunts, "You never catch my bullet."

The two leaders of ruthless desperados stare at the other and assess for any telling weakness. Bloody Ben sneers. "Nor you mine..."

A nearby Comanchero grabs hold of one of the girls and tries to pull her from the Indian pony. The girl screams wildly and lashes out. Black Hand steers his mount around Ben for a clearer view and nods his approval. "You bring us live ones this time!"

The girl is pulled, kicking and screaming, to the horseback Comanchero's side, and he buries his face in her neck to smell. With her bound hands, she grabs the man's knife from his belt and slashes the outlaw once, before stabbing the pointy blade deep in his thigh. He shrieks in pain and continues to hold the girl tightly to everyone's howling amusement. Blind with humiliation, the wounded outlaw draws his pistol, quickly cocks it, presses it to her chest and shoots the restrained prisoner.

All is quiet as the hostage girl falls limply to the ground in a dead heap. With pistol still smoking, the Comanchero looks around at everyone watching and shrugs his shoulders in an apologetic guilt. Bloody Ben looks to Black Hand, as the Indian raises his rifle from the hip and shoots toward the man at fault. The shamefaced Comanchero catches the bullet in the upper chest and spins from his mount to the ground next to the murdered girl.

The Comanche leader swings his leg forward over his animal's neck and slides from his horse. He strides up next to the wounded man, pulls the buried knife from his leg, then turns and looks to the others as they watch him with curiosity. In a thick almost Germanic accent, Black Hand addresses the onlookers in the white man's tongue.

"Everyone gets a try or no one does."

He reaches down, picks the offending man up by his long hair and pulls the knife across his exposed throat. Black Hand swipes back and forth, until he cuts through the flesh around the neck. He hacks twice at the spinal bone before severing it and then tosses the gruesome trophy at the feet of Bloody Ben's mount. "My apologies for your loss. You and your gifts are welcome in our camp."

Bloody Ben looks down at the separated head, nods and looks around at the current company. He grins and holsters his pistol at his side. "Good to be home."

Following the path of the other riders, Bloody Ben leads his two remaining horseback hostages down into the ravine and across a fork of the Brazos River.

Chapter 26

The trash-detail wagon rolls to a stop near two tied saddle horses under the broken shade of a tall mesquite tree. Private Dedman reaches back, tugs a string connected to the rear of the wagon, and the wooden tailgate flops down. From the concealed cavity under the rotting foodstuffs, Holton and Bear waste no time in wiggling free of the confined space.

The two buckskin-clad men stand next to the military support wagon and shake off the debris from the smuggled ride. Still atop the driver's box, Private Dedman grins, entertained, as they sniff their damp-spotted clothing and try to wipe the clinging smell of spoiled trash from themselves. "The Colonel said to load the juiciest scraps on the bottom to make y'all feel more comfortable."

Bear gives a coughing shiver. "This ain't gonna smell none too much better when the sun starts to cook on it."

Holton pats some food bits from his hat and looks up to the wagon box, as the Private lifts the big-loop rifle from a spot at his feet. Dedman holds out the special long gun and gives it a twirling spin-cock. The tip of the barrel swings within a hair's breadth of his cheek and his eyes go white as it comes around. Nearly frozen in shock, Dedman grips the rifle and looks down at Holton. "Whew! I's been wanting to do that since I saw yous win this repeater at that shootin' contest some time back."

"Not bad 'n better'n most."

Dedman grins and tosses the special rifle down to its owner. He looks over at the two saddled mounts tied nearby. "I know you probably don't be need'n my help, but I'd like to come along wit'cha."

Bear unties one of the horses, leads him away from the tree and looks to Holton, then Dedman. He hooks a thumb over his damp shoulder, back in the direction of Fort Davis. "What about the fort?"

Holton watches Dedman lean on the back ridge of the wagon seat and offers his concerned sentiments to the trooper. "We appreciate you helping us out of that bind, but we don't want to be liable for your desertion."

Private Dedman smiles and pats his upper vest pocket. "I's got a special dispensation from the Colonel hisself. He says to 'git Holton Lang and his trouble-making friend as far from this military post as possible' till he is gone from the command at the fort."

Holton walks to his horse in the shade and unties it. He looks to Bear, then up at the eager soldier atop the wagon bench. "Come along then. We may have some use of your marksmen skills with a long-gun when we catch up with Bloody Ben." Holton jumps a foot to the dangling stirrup, swings a leg over and mounts. The saddled gelding lifts its head high, as he is pulled around to face the others.

Bear puts his foot to his stirrup and climbs up on the mount alongside. "Why not? Holton, you's attract a mix of company like a barrel o' whiskey left 'hind the store house."

Mounted, they watch as Private Dedman uses a wide paddle stick to push back the garbage into a pile on the ground. Several wooden crates remain strapped in the wagon bed and Private Dedman steps over them gingerly as he climbs into the driver's box.

Holton directs his mount north, and Bear turns and follows. In the four wheeled cart, with a long-barreled, trapdoor Springfield rifle across his lap, the blue wool uniformed trooper slaps the reins on the mule team and turns the military wagon to follow after Holton and Bear.

~*~

Just across the border into Texas, a set of mud-brick ruins are the last remains of a homestead that was victim to Indian attacks years prior. As evening approaches, a healthy fire bounces light off the adobe block walls of the abandoned site. The crumbles of several broken structures can be made out from the far reaching glow.

Gimp Ear Walt stands near the window in the mostly roofless main building and looks out to the darkening landscape. He turns to Poncho, who attempts to cook a rabbit over the flames, then to their two captives, Jules and Alice. "Eh, Poncho, why don't you let the woman cook that?"

The Mexican glances up and finally gets the skinned rabbit carcass positioned properly over the fire.

"I know better than to let a wife or woman that wants me muerto cook for me."

Gimp Ear Walt leans on the wooden window frame and looks to his saddle pal inquisitively. "You been married?"

"Sí, three times." Poncho smiles and pulls his knife from the ground where it was stuck near his boot. He looks to Alice and makes a sweeping slash with the sharp blade near his neck. "They all tried to kill me, but I get them first."

Walt's eyes go wide as he stares at Poncho in disbelief. "Jeez, all three of them?"

Jules shifts nearer Alice in attempt to shield her, and the boy's eyes peer over at Poncho as he mumbles quietly, "You're kinder hard on wives."

The Mexican man, squatted near the flames, holds the weapon as he stares at Jules and smiles wide. "You are young yet and do not know the ways of women. They will try to kill you one way or another." He wags his glistening knife at Alice. "I can see it in her eyes that she would murder me in a second if given the chance."

The captive woman looks away, hugging her knees to her chest, and Poncho continues his lecturing rant on matrimony. "You will not live long boy, but they say it is better to have loved and lost … yes, tis better." Poncho laughs uproariously and sits back on his heels nearly to the large roweled spurs on his boots. A glimpse of movement in the night catches Gimp Ear Walt's attention and he stares out into the deepening shadows. He waves a hand to quiet Poncho and whispers, "Shh, I thought I saw something out there."

"It is just that ugly dog still creeping about."

Walt glances back at his partner. "Could be Injuns …"

The Mexican spits to the side of the crackling flames around the cooking rabbit. "I will go out later and kill that dog for breakfast." Poncho grins and looks to Jules. "How would you like that, boy?"

"I don't eat dog."

"Have you tried it? I will make you eat this one after I have the girl skin and cook it." Amused with himself, Poncho laughs and twirls his knife. He looks to Walt pacing near the window and shakes his head. "You have the eyesight of a badger and can no hear good with that stub on yer head."

The outlaw at the window watches the three horses nearby as they perk their ears to the slight breeze.

"The horses hear something."

"You gimp-eared half-wit, what are we going to do, eh? Sit up all night and watch for Indians? There are Comanche all over, from here to the Brazos. If you see one, shoot it!"

Walt holds Jules' Mexican decorated Sharps rifle and sits down in an old, half-broke chair by the dark window opening. He mumbles quietly to himself, "I don't want my other ear cut off by savages."

Poncho plops down by the campfire with a jingle of spurs and looks to the young captives backed up against one of the broken adobe walls.

"You two stick close, there are Injuns out there in the night who won't treat you as nice as us."

The Mexican laughs at his own astute remark, as the fire's flames lick up at the long, lean form of the cooking rabbit. Jules watches and studies the weapons on each of his captors. He glances across the room to his Walker pistol tucked near the set of saddle bags and waits for the right circumstance to make a grab for it.

Chapter 27

The fire has died down to a rolling glow inside the adobe cabin as the Mexican carves into the cooked rabbit. He tosses a skinny leg toward Walt and looks up to Jules and Alice.

"Hungry?"

Poncho cuts off the head of the rabbit with its singed ears and tosses it at the boy's feet. Jules stares back at the Mexican until Alice reaches down and picks up the charred head. She pulls off a tiny piece of meat and offers it to Jules. He eats the scrap, and Poncho laughs as he sits back and eats from the sinewy, roasted carcass.

"You don't eat dog. Hah! You surely will when you get hungry enough, caballero."

Gimp Ear Walt finishes the scant meat on the long scrawny leg of the rabbit and, unsatisfied, turns to Poncho. "Toss me more of that jackrabbit."

"Why? You no killed it nor cooked it. I was being generous before with what you got."

The gaunt, one-eared outlaw looks downcast and hungry as he stares at the picked clean leg-bone in hand. "I was standing guard duty."

"From what?"

Watching Poncho eat the remainder of the carcass, Walt stands awkwardly at the window and utters, "I thought we'd share."

"I did already. Go share with them."

Walt looks over to Alice picking cooked skin from the rabbit head then rubs his thin, grumbling belly. He tosses the leg aside and marches over to the hostages. Grabbing the rabbit head by the burnt ears, he puts the empty eye socket to his mouth and sucks at the tiny, cooked brain.

An arrow swishes into the glowing light inside the adobe ruins and pierces through the side of Walt's neck. He tosses the rabbit head away and screams in terror as his eyes try to focus on the arrow shaft stuck between his collarbone and jaw. Several more Indian arrows bounce into the ruins and Poncho rolls away while pulling his sidearm.

Jules sees an opportunity, pushes Alice against the wall and scrambles for his Walker pistol by the saddle gear. The Mexican outlaw stands nearby and delivers a brutish kick to the young boy that sends him tumbling across the dirt floor, gasping for breath. Without aiming at anything, Poncho fires his pistol out the dark window and the muzzle flash of ignited gunpowder fills the room with a blinding light and smoke.

Gimp Ear Walt goes into panic as he runs around the campfire howling in pain. He tries unsuccessfully to pull out the blood-slicked arrow poking completely through his neck. "Get it out!"

Poncho kicks at the biggest log in the campfire, shoots his gun into the darkness and yells over his shoulder toward Walt, "Git down you fool…"

He fires another indiscriminate shot as Gimp Ear Walt stops his running and sits weeping against a half-crumpled mud brick wall. A quiet moment passes as the scattered campfire slowly dies down. Jules regains his breath and watches Poncho crouched by the window across the room. He looks over at Walt who whimpers like a small animal, as blood flows from his neck wound down his shirtfront.

The silence is deafening as the remaining campfire breaks down to glowing coals that occasionally lick flames into the night. Poncho reloads his pistol and stares out the window into the faint surrounding moonlight outside. He looks back to the room and assesses the situation of his useless, wounded partner and two captives. In the dimness, his eyes connect with Jules, and he smiles as he motions to the Walker pistol laid out on the floor. "Good luck, hijo…"

Snapping off another gunshot into the outside darkness, Poncho leaps through the window and disappears into the veiling shadows.

Moving past the glowing embers of fire, Jules crawls to the Walker pistol and checks the firearm for loaded chambers. The shiny gleam of percussion caps staggered at the rear of the cylinder reassures him and he cocks the hammer back. He moves over to a set of familiar saddlebags and rummages through for bullet lead, caps and loose powder, then scoots across the floor, returning to Alice's side.

From the window opening across the room from the dying campfire, a loose arrow rattles across the floor near Jules and another Comanche arrow pierces Walt's leg. The second inflicted injury sends Gimp Ear Walt into another howling spasm of pain. Jules turns to face a shadowed figure looking through a window in the dim firelight and fires off a shot from the large horse pistol. The .44 caliber lead slams into the Comanche brave dead-center and sends him tumbling back from the framed opening out into the cool darkness.

Squatted at Alice's side, Jules opens the powder bag and quickly reloads the spent chamber. All is quiet in the fading glow of burning coals from the campfire at the center of the room. The only sound in the chill starry night is the snort of horses in the corral and the pained crying whimper of Gimp Ear Walt.

~*~

The sun begins to inch over the horizon on the wide plains of West Texas. Following a trail, Holton and Bear ride horseback alongside each other followed by

Private Dedman driving the wagon. The men study a mix of pony tracks in the dirt, and Holton steps down from his mount to examine them.

Bear grunts, as his features glow in the early morning sunrise. "Comanche?"

"Could be, there's a mess of 'em."

"They on the same trail we're following?"

"Yeah."

The wagon pulls up, and Private Dedman eases the mule team to an ambling stop. He looks at Holton beside the tracks on the trail, then to Bear, still astride his mount. "Injuns ya figure?"

Bear nods and utters, "Possibly Comanche."

The uniformed private shakes his head slowly and sighs. "Comanche or Apache, don't make no difference to me. An angry Indian will do terrible things." Dedman lifts his short-bill McClellan cap and runs his hand over his smooth shaved head.

Bear smiles his bearded grin. "Hell, they ought to leave that scalp alone, 'less they want to skin a cannonball." The burly scout scratches his own gray whiskers and grunts, "They could make a nice rug for all the hair I got on me."

Dedman nods with a smile. "With all the buffalo gone, yers is the next best thing."

Bear nods his agreement and tries to lighten the mood as he shifts in the saddle.

"Hey, there Holton, don't you go saying nothin' 'bout the seasoned smell either."

Holton glances at Bear, and their gaze connects with a discerning assessment to the seriousness of the followed trail. He toes his boot in the dirt, looks ahead and steps back into the saddle. They prod their horses onward with the wagon rolling along behind, the three remaining ever-watchful of the potentially hostile environment to come.

~*~

The early morning sun sends bright rays of daylight in through the broken adobe walls. Settled back in the corner with an easy view of the door and windows, Alice holds the Sharps rifle and Jules keeps the large horse pistol propped on his knee, cocked and ready. In a moment of eerie silence, the breeze blows calm and nothing is heard, with exception of Walt's panting breath.

Suddenly, the room erupts into action. The sharpened flint tip of an arrow explodes a chunk of hard adobe over Jules' head and he fires at a Comanche warrior passing outside the doorway. Another flying arrow pierces through Gimp Ear Walt's wrist, and he screams anew.

Alice raises the rifle and shoots at a dark figure running by a low broken wall, and he stumbles then drops from view. With the pistol cocked again, Jules scans the empty doorway and windows then waits. "Reload that rifle, Ma'am."

Alice breaks open the rifle's breach, ejects the smoking brass casing and pulls a fresh cartridge from the ammo belt. While Alice reloads, two more Comanche rush over the short wall outside the cabin. Jules fires once, cocks slowly and shoots again, hitting the second Comanche, knocking him down. The remaining Indian stands silhouetted in the open doorway and screams a blood curdling war-cry while raising his rifle aim toward Jules and Alice. Walt wails in horrified agony as both guns explode simultaneously.

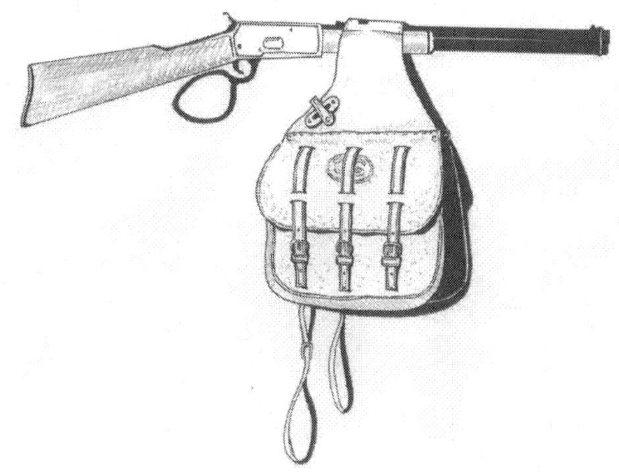

Chapter 28

In the far distance, the faint pop of gunfire is heard and Holton and Bear halt their horses. In the early daylight, they stand stopped in their tracks. They strain to listen, looking to each other with the same question before glancing back to Private Dedman, behind with the military wagon.

Coming over the horizon at full tilt, they watch as Dog races toward them. The lean body of the canine stretches out with his head pointed forward like an arrow. Bear looks from the sprinting animal to Holton and grunts, "I thought that dog was finally rid of you."

"He was with the boy."

"Looks to be that's where he wants us to go."

Both men sink spur and lunge their mounts forward. Far ahead, Dog stops in the trail and gives a howling yelp skyward and then turns back, leading the way. Private Dedman stands in the driver's box, slaps the reins and urges the wagon team along at a trotting pace.

~*~

Inside the broken adobe cabin, Jules fires off another pistol shot, and a Comanche brave ducks away near the dead Indian at the doorway. The boy puts the bag of reloading supplies to his lap and speaks quietly to the woman beside him. "Hold yer shot Alice, till I finish my reload."

"There's one just outside!"

"Hold the shot and make it count …"

Alice gives Jules a sidelong glimpse, as she keeps her attention on the cabin entrance and windows. The boy tips his revolver barrel skyward and measures a load of black powder. He pours the loose grains into the big cylinder and places a lead ball on top before ramming the loading lever down with both hands. With the lead slug firmly seated, he quickly places a percussion cap on the loaded cylinder nipple and repeats the process with the other spent chambers.

Alice holds the rifle steady, fearful, yet patient as the taunting cries of Comanche warriors echo outside. The sound of the horses being gathered from the adobe corral catches their attention, and Alice moves to stand. Jules puts his arm out to stop her and shakes his head side to side.

"Let the horses go. Maybe they'll leave us be."

"We won't make it far without horses."

"Better off than being dead …" Jules rams the last lead ball down in the chamber and gestures to Alice as a Comanche warrior rises from the brush outside. She shoulders the rifle, takes quick aim and fires. The rushing Indian holds a readied carbine across his chest as he continues running toward them. Jules quickly places the last percussion cap on the cylinder and pulls the hammer back on the big handgun.

As the screaming Comanche advances with a leap through the window, Jules jerks the trigger and the handgun roars with a chain-fire of four chambers. The startled warrior takes three .44 caliber slugs in the torso and the Walker pistol kicks back, flying out of Jules' grip. Alice hurriedly tries to reload the rifle and looks up as several more painted Indians rush the adobe structure.

The sound of their stolen horses galloping away is suddenly displaced by the sound of several charging mounts approaching the fight. Out in front of the cabin, a shot fires and one of the Comanche warriors tumbles aside as the buckskin figure of Holton Lang on horseback appears through the framed doorway. Holton spin-cocks his big-loop lever rifle and fires to the side, as Bear rides past at a hard gallop, shooting his pistol.

Another Comanche crawls through the window as Alice reloads the rifle. He comes forward menacingly with his war club held high. A growling snap is heard as Dog leaps over a low, crumbled wall and grabs hold of the native's wrist. With a thrashing snarl, the canine shakes the threatening club from the Indian's grip.

A shot explodes from Alice's rifle and the Comanche yowls as the bullet passes through his side.

He shakes off the vicious attacking dog and quickly dashes out the cabin door. Dog stands protectively snarling at the doorway as Jules grabs up his Walker pistol again and resumes reloading.

The gunshots and horseback action outside begin to fade away, and the wheeled sound of a wagon rattling past takes their place. Jules looks across the interior of the partial cabin, as Holton's horse leaps over one of the low broken walls and tromps through the dead coals of the fire circle in the room. Seated high in the roofless dwelling, Holton levers his rifle and scans the adobe ruins. The horseback figure looks down at the unharmed captives in the process of reloading their guns, and an overwhelming sense of surprised relief surges through him.

"Good to see you're both still alive!" He steals a glance toward Alice, who, doe-eyed, watches him a moment, then looks away. As his horse turns, he spots another Comanche leap from the brush nearby and puts the big-loop rifle to his shoulder and fires. He levers the gun again and hops from the saddle. "Put that horse pistol aside and get to shootin', boy."

Holton gives his horse a slap on the rump and directs it toward the far corner. He pulls his single-action Army Colt revolver with a spinning gesture and tosses it to Jules, who catches it in his lap. Watching the boy take a gun in each hand, he shakes his head incredulously before kneeling near a low tumbled wall of mud bricks.

The boy grips both pistols in hand and crawls to a window near Holton. He looks out to see Bear on horseback, chasing the fleeing Comanche up toward the rising terrain in the west. The remaining Indians scramble from the brush toward a group of waiting war ponies near the ridge.

The rattle and wood-creaking rumble of the supply wagon turns Jules' attention, and he watches a dark-skinned US Cavalry soldier swing the mule team around and lock the brake wheel of the wagon to a skidding stop. The remaining Indian braves take to horse and flee in every direction, as Bear, with a contented but watchful eye lopes his horse back to the adobe ruins. As the kicked up dust finally settles around the cabin, the hostilities appear to be over. Holton leaves his saddled horse inside the cabin walls and steps out to greet Bear.

The burly scout reins up his mount and surveys the homestead. "We done a fair bit of damage 'n run 'em off."

"Catch any of them ponies?"

Bear grins down at Holton. "They sure baited 'em 'n wanted me to ... but then they was gonna catch me."

Holton stares away to the horizon, on the lookout for another attack. "No matter, they can ride in the wagon."

Bear looks over at the cabin, with the boy standing alone in the window, holding the two pistols. He moves his horse nearer toward Holton and lowers his voice a bit. "What's that, ya say? Both of 'em still alive yet?"

Holton glances toward the cabin with a nod, then looks up to Private Dedman, still atop the wagon seat. "Private, mind taking that long rifle of yours and watching them hills for hostiles?"

Lifting the .50-70 trapdoor Springfield from the wagon, Dedman climbs down and smiles. He cradles the long wooden stock over his arm and grabs his loaded ammo belt from the wagon seat. With a studied stare to the landscape, the trooper resumes his friendly grin. "Don't mind at all."

The Buffalo Soldier jogs over and positions himself behind one of the perimeter adobe walls. Settled in, with the ammunition supply spread out along the top of the crumbling bricks, Dedman licks his finger and touches his front aiming sight. He puts the rifle to his shoulder to scan the distant hills.

Jules steps from the remains of the adobe cabin, holding the Walker pistol in one hand and Holton's sidearm in the other. He holds out the borrowed pistol toward Holton and lifts his chin. "Thank you, Mister Lang … for the loaner."

Holton takes the firearm, opens the side gate, ejects the spent casings and reloads fresh cartridges from his holster belt. Bear remains in the saddle, circles his horse and looks at the many dead warriors sprawled out around the adobe structure and surrounding area. "Boy… you done a good bit of fighting with that old-fashioned hand-cannon."

Jules looks up at the horseback figure and nods. "Yes, Sir. I intend to do a bit more 'fore I put it to rest."

Bear swings down from his mount and exchanges an admiring glance with Holton. The bearded military scout walks nearer the cabin and gestures toward Gimp Ear Walt on the floor at the back wall of the structure. He stares through the window at the semi-conscious, wounded outlaw.

"Who's the other one in there?"

Jules holds the Walker pistol cradled in both his small hands. The boy turns to the adobe cabin entryway and motions for the men to follow.

"C'mon, I'll show you."

The young man enters the broke-down, mud-brick structure, with Holton and Bear coming along behind.

Chapter 29

Inside the adobe ruins, Holton's horse stands in the corner and waits patiently. Jules takes hold of the bridle, leads the horse to the side chamber and gently brushes off the soot-covered feet. He gives the animal a pat on the flank and moves back to where Gimp Ear Walt sits slumped against the wall. Jules glances toward Alice, who watches with the loaded Sharps rifle in hand.

Holton and Bear approach the boy from the doorway, and Jules reports to them from the middle of the room. "He's the only one left here. The other Mexican fella run off in the dark when the fight came."

Holton stands over Walt, looking down at the bloody mess coming from his neck wound and the arrow piercing his leg. The injured outlaw looks up with the whites of his eyes and whimpers feebly, "Kill me … please."

The room is quiet as Holton gazes around the broke down, abandoned cabin. Moving toward the window, Bear leans against the jamb and turns away to look out at the hills. Alice steps outside, still holding the Sharps rifle across her chest, and Holton's focus finally falls on the young boy.

"Was he one of the men who killed yer family?"

Jules takes a step forward, and his whole body visibly trembles as he glares down at Walt.

"Yes Sir, he was."

Holton nods understandingly and gestures at Gimp Ear Walt. "You can kill 'em if you'd like."

Jules stands before Walt with the Walker pistol griped tightly in front of him. The weight of the large gun weighs heavy in his small hands as Walt looks up at the young boy.

"Do it, kid."

Jules clenches his teeth and slowly pulls back the hammer with a slow series of clicks that turns the cylinder. Walt lifts his head and a squirt of fresh blood oozes from the neck wound. The dying outlaw smiles at the boy and groans, "I'm already dead …"

After a long moment, Jules shakes his head. "I don't think I'd care to."

Holton puts his hand on the boy's shoulder and gives it a paternal squeeze, as a proud feeling of moral integrity swells up inside. Holton stands next to the boy and clenches his jaw to conceal the emotion. "Let's go find yer sisters."

Gimp Ear Walt leans forward, struggles on the ground and reaches out for Jules. "Damn you, boy! Someone have mercy!"

Holton escorts Jules toward the door, and Walt screams out with his last waning gush of energy. "I killed your family dammit! Cut 'em down and murdered them all … Don't that mean nothing to ya?"

The blast of a rifle shot fills the room with a plume of gray smoke, and Jules spins to face the outlaw as a bullet smashes into the open mouth of the dying man. Holton and Jules both look over to see Alice leaning inside one of the wood-framed window openings with the Mexican Sharps rifle in hand. She stares blankly ahead a moment, then looks at them with tears streaming down her face. "He done more'n that …"

Holton steps around the broken adobe wall, stands before Alice and watches her, not knowing how to offer comfort. He reaches out to take the rifle from her grasp, but she holds it tight. She looks up at the buckskin-clad man with a hard stare, smears tears from her cheek and turns away. "Don't pity me none. I'll survive these bastards yet."

Alice moves away, holding the rifle and ammunition belt as she walks to the wagon. Holton senses Jules close behind him and turns to glance at the boy. They both watch Alice climb into the wagon and sit, with the rifle across her lap, on the wooden crate in the shallow bed. There is a visible quiver to her shoulders as she sobs silently and reloads the rifle. All is quiet as Bear stands at the window and Dedman stares off to the hills.

Jules watches the emotionally damaged woman in the wagon and speaks aside. "Neither of us is gonna give up or stop till they're all dead on the ground."

Holton looks down to the young man, and Jules moves to the wagon, holding the Walker pistol cradled against his chest. Standing alone near the entrance to the broken adobe ruins, Holton turns his gaze to Bear, then Dedman. He takes a deep understanding breath and murmurs, "Yeah ..."

~*~

Parked in front of the derelict adobe cabin, the military escort wagon is loaded with extra saddle gear packed around the lone wooden crate. Alice sits comfortably in the back, and Jules waits on the driver's bench with the Walker pistol resting on his knee. Leading his saddle mount out from the adobe ruins, Holton calls out to Dedman, "Private, ready to move out?"

The dark-skinned trooper remains crouched down with his rifle aimed toward the hills. He holds up a finger to signal for silence. In a quiet whisper, barely audible to the others, the Buffalo Soldier speaks, almost to himself. "I's seen three of 'em prowlers jest o'er that rise. Saw the tips of the ponies' ears..."

Bear stands next to his horse and leads it closer to the wagon. "Well, let's go 'n git 'fore they get any queer ideas."

Holton looks to a dead Comanche brave rolled against one of the low adobe walls. "We've nearly got the numbers evened out. Most likely jest hanging 'round to gather their dead."

Private Dedman keeps his keen eye trained along the sights of his rifle as he speaks. "They's can jest wait till we're gone ..."

Holton stares off to the horizon along the sighted direction. "Could be they stay on our trail awhile and wait for an advantaged opportunity."

In the far distance, the horseback figures of three Comanche warriors can be seen through the waves of heat coming from the scrub covered ground. Bear spits aside and pats his horse along the neck. "Nothing to be done with 'em at that distance."

With the long-gun pointed skyward, Dedman targets the rifle. "We'll see 'bout that."

The sharp-eyed trooper squeezes the trigger, waits a moment for the sound of the rifle shot to reverberate away and stands. The breeze wafts away the smoke from the gunshot, and Bear climbs into the saddle. He takes up the leather reins and grunts as he begins to turn his horse away. "T'was a longer shot than our reach."

Suddenly, the Indian on the left drops from his pony, and the others retreat their mounts and disappear from the horizon. Bear's bearded jaw drops in stunned disbelief. "I'll be damned …"

Holton gives an impressed whistle and steps up to the saddle. "Yer a better shot than I've e'er seen, Private."

Dedman reloads with a smile and strolls to the wagon. He puts his index finger up to the breeze to test for direction. "Good thing there were three of 'em lined up. I sure won't tell ya which I was a aimin' at."

Private Dedman hands his trapdoor Springfield rifle up to Jules and climbs into the driver's box. The young man looks to the hills, down at the long gun and leans over to the black cavalry trooper. "Wow, I never seen someone take a shot like that."

"Twarn't much. Was nobody shootin' back at me."

"The hell you say? That was a heck of a shot."

The Buffalo Soldier smiles and nods toward Holton. "You see ol' Holton Lang there in action, and you'll have seen something alright." Dedman unloops the leather lead lines from the break lever and gives the harness team a slap of the reins. "I seen him in a runnin' fight, horseback, with a hundred Apache all around, and he was a'twirling that rifle like a windmill. Next thing ya know, he's headed off into the rocky hills by hisself, after the worst Apache renegade known in them parts."

The wagon lunges forward, and the trooper peeks over his shoulder to see that he has both Jules' and Alice's keen interest on the subject. He shakes his head as he looks toward Holton riding away on horseback. "Nobody, 'cept Holton Lang could follow an Apache into the rocks alone and even think ta come out alive."

The team circles around, and Dedman steers the wagon to follow along behind Bear and Holton as they travel west toward the canyons on the Brazos.

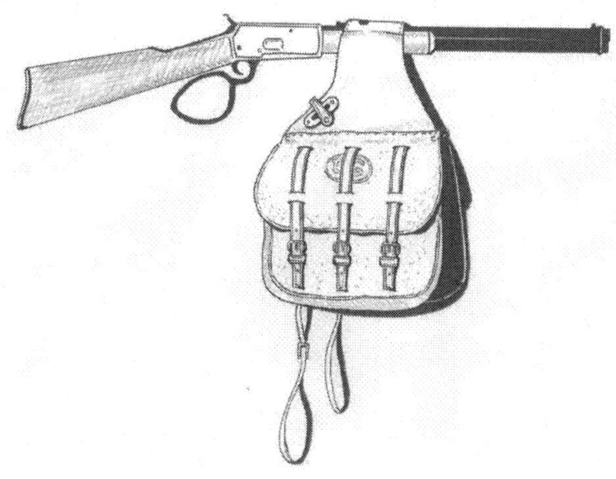

Chapter 30

The military wagon, led by two buckskin men on horseback and a rangy dog, travels toward the Brazos river basin. Holton and Bear watch their surroundings and study the ground as they ride along with Dog at their heels. The unusual grouping of companions covers miles of desolate country as they travel north. The flat dry plains of West Texas start to give way to the rolling hills and canyon breaks of the Llano Estacado.

Bear watches as Holton dismounts and inspects several tracks on the silty, dirt ground ahead, then looks around, apprehensive. The burly scout on horseback adjusts in the saddle and shakes his head in a show of discouragement.

"You followin' any trail in particular?"

"There is a fresh one here mixed with the rest. Could lead us where we're going … or not."

Bear looks back to the wagon following a short distance behind and lowers his voice as he speaks to Holton. "Ya think those sisters of his are even still alive?"

Holton swings himself back into the saddle seat and glances over at Bear. "Could be …"

Bear tongues the chaw in his cheek and spits aside. "Don't make no nevermind to the kid, I suppose. He's gonna want to find 'n see 'em either way." Holton nods solemnly and nudges his horse onward.

~*~

At the base of a rough scrub and tree-lined canyon, the Comanchero camp is a ramshackle mix of stick cabins, stone huts and partially shaded areas. A steady trickle of water runs near the center of the camp along a hard rock span of riverbed that spreads over a dozen feet wide and a few inches deep. The area is scattered with neglected belongings along with food trash and whiskey bottles.

The lone, horseback figure of Bloody Ben appears at the tree-line near the escarpment to the upper plateau. He rides his mount down a steep trail and trots into the secluded canyon below. A roughly constructed horse corral sits at the far end of the camp and he rides toward it and dismounts.

Ben unsaddles his animal and throws his saddle near a pile of discarded horse tack. He holds his rifle and walks toward the log and stone structures randomly placed around the area. In the hot, still air, Bloody Ben stops and looks around the vacant camp before entering one of the poorly constructed stone huts through a dirty, woven-blanket door.

~*~

Holton pulls back on the reins to hold his mount up and looks out over the many canyons formed by the deeply trenched tributaries feeding into the Brazos River. He watches the birds overhead and listens to the emptiness of the breeze.

Bear stops his horse beside and scans the varied landscape which seems devoid of human activity. "That's a lot of territory to cover."

Holton peers over his near shoulder toward the mule-hitched wagon as it rolls up at the edge of the bluff. "Ain't gonna be possible to explore all them gullies with that wagon setup and passengers."

The military wagon, driven by Private Dedman, with the boy and the woman in back, draws up and stops. Jules stands in the shallow wagon bed and looks out over the canyons below.

"How do we get down there?"

Holton pulls his studied gaze from the broken terrain and looks back at Jules. "You don't."

"The hell you say!"

Bear lifts an eyebrow at the young man's conviction and Holton turns his chin. "We've lost the trail. It would be best to split parties and search from both the top and bottom."

Jules looks around a moment then starts to move to the edge of the wagon bed. "I ain't staying in this wheel cart." The young man reaches down and seizes up his large horse pistol. He stands at the side of the wagon with the oversized shooter against his chest and stares eye to eye with Holton. "Them two outlaws said they were going to meet up at the canyons of Seven Fingers a' Brazos 'nd this looks to be it."

The young man has a hard determined look in his eye that Holton has become all too familiar with. Jules stares at the horseback men and speaks his mind. "I ain't gonna sit and wait behind. I'll just follow you and Bear on foot wherever you go, alongside Dog."

Holton looks out over the rough terrain and sighs, "You're a tough kid, but you ain't gonna be able to keep up with us being horseback." He watches the young man, with the large Walker pistol, grab his bag of reloading supplies and climb down from the wagon. Jules walks up to Holton and stands his tallest. He stares skyward, while Dog trots from the shade of the mule team and sits at the boy's side. "I'm going with you, like it or not."

Private Dedman smiles his friendly, familiar grin and leans down, putting an elbow to a knee. "That boy has sure got ample gumption."

Alice sits at the back of the wagon with the Sharps rifle across her lap. She looks toward Jules and calls out to Holton, "I don't see how you're going to stop us, Mister Lang!"

Holton looks over to the woman in the wagon and then to Bear. The older grizzled scout scratches his chin whiskers and thinks a moment before stepping off his mount. "The lady is correct, Holton. I don't see much use in wastin' our breath." With a sweeping gesticulated wave, Bear motions Jules over to his saddled horse. "Hop aboard 'n dangle them skinny legs astride, son. You've got some rough terrain ahead of ya."

They all watch as Jules nimbly climbs aboard Bear's sweated mount and gets himself situated in the saddle with the trusted, Walker handgun. Holton prods with his spurred boot heels, steering his horse closer to Jules, and reaches back into his leather saddle bags.

"Put that damn horse pistol away …"

Holton pulls out the ivory-handled six-shooter from the dead Mexican and gives it a twirl on his finger. "Tuck that in yer britches and have it at the quick if we get to needin' it."

Bear stands next to Jules and pats his leg. "You listen to Holton there. That shooter is a whole lot easier to load and a touch faster at the hammer."

The independent and often solitary individual, Holton Lang, looks out over his random mix of company and snorts. In his many years of living with the Apache and scouting for the military, he had never felt such odd closeness of family as he did now. He reaches down and makes sure his big-loop rifle is seated firm in the scabbard and looks up at his devoted assembly. "We'll check the lower regions and you can stay atop and work yer way around the bluffs to the north and east. We'll do what we can to keep in sight on toward dusk."

Holton turns his horse and looks over the steep ledge to the river bottom below. "You coming, boy?"

"Yes, sir."

Jules puts the fancy pistol in his waistband and tucks the long barreled Walker handgun back between the cantle and the secured blanket-roll. He kicks his legs, prodding the horse forward, and pushes past Holton. The young man maneuvers the horse over the brink of the rock face and slides the mount down the embankment toward the canyon floor.

Bear laughs, as they watch the young man cling to the saddle while lying back clear to the horse's rump. "Holton, you jest make sure to keep up with that young sprout. He's green 'nough not to know any better!"

Holton looks to Dedman, who offers a casual salute, then back at Bear. They exchange a cautious look, and Holton turns his horse to the precipitous trail down. With Dog following, Holton drops his horse over the edge of the cliff and slides the steep terrain to the tree-lined canyon below.

~*~

At the top of the Llano Estacado, in the far remoteness, a single horseback figure moves out quick and rides hard with a dusty cloud trailing. The whirling of horse hooves gives off a steady drumming patter on the dry, dusty terrain. As the unified figure gallops closer, the blur of man and horse is barely discernable, with the exception of the distinct glinting shine from a pair of fancy Mexican spurs.

Not far behind, on Poncho's fleeing back-trail, another grouping of several riders charges after him. The pursuing chase races horseback across wide open Texas landscape. The larger group is slowly gaining and occasionally firing off rifle shots, sending puffs of gray smoke skyward.

Approaching a small chasm ahead, Poncho frantically slaps the dangling tails of his leather reins on the horse's flank, urging it to leap him over the gaping void. He looks back, as the nearing group of pursuers hesitates, then splits ranks. Half of the riders leap the gorge and the other half swing around to the north.

The single rider gallops away and rides a short distance to another steep embankment. Poncho jerks his mount's head back at the mouth in a spray of foaming lather and looks down at the brink. He scans the treacherous descent below and maneuvers his heaving animal alongside the edge, searching for a less steep access down. The Mexican glimpses back at the band of pursuers gaining ground and ducks as several bullets whirl overhead.

"You's bastards ..."

Loping his fatigued horse along the narrow ridge, Poncho rides too close and the frail ground gives way under the animal's faltering hooves. They both hang mid-air for a short moment before Poncho cartwheels down the escarpment face in a whirl of horse, rider and tumbling earth.

Chapter 31

The loose, scrub-rooted edge of the cliff crumbles as rock and debris roll down into the canyon below. Poncho slides to the bottom as his horse rolls over the saddle then awkwardly finds its feet again. The dusty, earth-covered Mexican takes a step toward the startled animal and reaches out for the headstall. Just as Poncho grasps the halter, he trips on one of his long, spur shanks and the horse bolts sideways, running away down the canyon.

"Git back here ya damned beast!"

The clop of a single horse running away echoes down the hollow ravine. The lonely sound is quickly replaced by the cadence of several horseback riders approaching from the opposite direction. Poncho dusts off his shoulder and waits.

Several troopers, in trail-dusted, blue wool uniforms, ride up with Sergeant Kilbern in the lead. The horse soldiers angle their lathered and sweat-streaked mounts in a semi-circle around Poncho, who stands afoot. Kilbern raises his pistol at the tousled Mexican before them and calls out to his men, "If he tries to run, shoot his legs out from under him."

Poncho looks down to his pistol still in his holster. He carefully draws it out with two fingers, holds it forward and tosses it toward the Sergeant.

"I no like to run afoot."

The Mexican bandit humorously holds up one of his boot heels with the large spur rowel and gives the spiked metal disk a whirl. He studies each soldier faced-off to him and turns back to Sergeant Kilbern.

"I don't think I know you … do I?"

"No, but I know your type."

"I am just a lonely traveler."

Sergeant Kilbern nudges his horse forward and stares down at Poncho before him, standing on the ground. "We are on the trail of a recently escaped murderer who goes by the name of Holton Lang."

Poncho looks up at the Sergeant on horseback.

"Is there a fort near to here?"

"We rode out from Fort Tularosa."

"You are a long way from home and in Texas, Señor." The Mexican pats some of the acquired filth from his clothing in a puff of white dust and thinks a long moment. "Could he be a buckskin muchacho who rides after a boy and spins a long-arm?"

"That's the one."

"I do not know where he is exactly at this moment, but I do know where he will be going."

The sergeant stares down at Poncho, then looks around at his horseback troopers, before responding, "Will you take us to him?"

"What do I get for helping you?" Poncho squints an eye cunningly. "Cuanto dinero?"

Sergeant Kilbern raises his already-cocked pistol and directs it at Poncho's upturned head. "We won't shoot you down right here."

Poncho looks around and watches as several more soldiers ride down the canyon with his sequestered horse in tow. He shrugs his shoulders and stares up at the Sergeant. "If I lead you to him, I am free to ride out?"

"Yes."

A smile curls at the edges of the Mexican's lips, and Poncho pats more dust from his sleeve.

"Sí, you have a deal."

~*~

The bottomlands along the Brazos river basin are rocky and tree-scrub filled canyons. Holton and Jules ride in single file through the uneven terrain, as Dog picks his way along on either side. The wind rattles the leaves in the trees, and Holton reins in his horse and listens.

Jules nudges his mount closer and shakes his head despondently. "We ain't going to find anyone in these narrows." The experienced tracker raises his hand for silence and searches along the craggy bluffs overhead. He listens a while to seeming nothingness and nods to the boy.

"Cain't see far, but the sound of a horse on the river bottom will carry a distance against these rock walls." Holton walks his horse to the edge of the meandering stream of water that flows through the canyon and lets his animal lower its head to drink. Jules eases alongside and listens into the still, quiet air.

"I don't hear any horses."

Holton stares at nothing in particular as he lets his surroundings carry the focused direction of his hearing. "You're not listening for horses. Hear the sounds an animal makes when they move through the area."

Jules looks at Holton, confused. "Which is?"

"The tumble of rocks ... the splash of water."

The young student listens awhile then shakes his head. "I don't hear any of that."

The drinking horse raises its mouth from the stream and Holton steers him along the watery path. The tracker's gaze remains fixed ahead, as Jules urges his horse to follow.

"Neither do I," Holton murmurs over his shoulder as he continues on.

~*~

The sound of thundering hooves echoes through the canyon, as Black Hand and his twenty Comanchero renegades ride down the steep slope and burst into camp. A blanketed door opens to one of the stone huts and Bloody Ben steps out, shirtless, into the mid-day sun. He looks to Black Hand and his crew, as they ride close with several fresh scalps hanging from their fighting lances.

"Where the hell have you been?"

Black Hand whirls his horse and grins merrily. "Out making war ... not laying with broken girls who were a white man's Indian gift."

Ben looks around at the motley mob of mixed-breed riders and their Comanche leader. "I won 'em back in fair game. I would have preferred cash money. They're still for sale if ya want 'em."

"You deal a crooked hand, like all your kind."

Bloody Ben rubs his hairy chest and spits. A slight trickle of blood oozes from his cheek wound were a fresh scratch tore off the healing scab. He stares up at the horseback group gathered around and speaks loud for all to hear. "You make fight on penniless farmers with homes in the dirt. The worthy prize is with big wagon trains."

Black Hand places his palm on his chest over the blood-smeared symbol of his name. "I make fight and kill any white-eyes putting homes on our native land. Me thinks you might die next!"

Ben looks down at his empty hip where his pistol and gun-belt usually hang. His hands hang at his side, and his gaze travels over to the blanketed cabin door. He looks back up to Black Hand and speaks cautiously. "We have been friends for many years."

The crazed Comanche leader glares down at the white man. "Leaders of men have no friends, only enemies in hiding. I should like to kill you someday!"

Black Hand flashes his teeth, as he wheels his horse and whoops a high-pitched war cry. Ben steps back to the doorway of the stone hut and glances at the rifle propped inside the frame. He watches the other Comanche renegades gallop their painted war ponies around camp, waving their bloody trophies and screaming in celebrated unison.

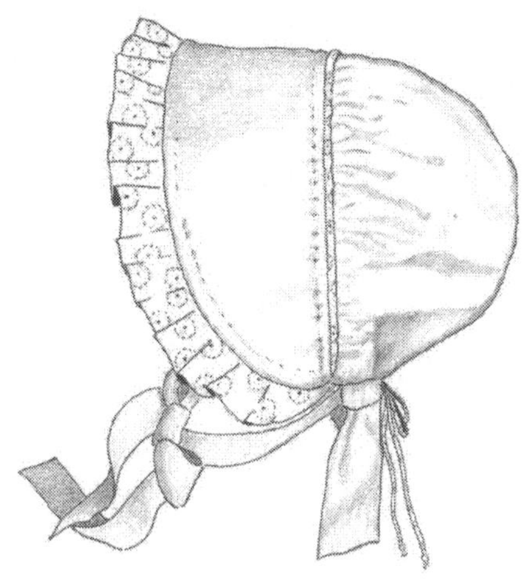

Chapter 32

The loud celebration in the Comanchero camp carries on into the latter part of the day. Not far off down the canyon, Holton and Jules leave their horses tied and walk carefully along the wide path of the riverbed. Concealed in the brush, they creep closer to the lively camp and observe.

Jules eyes the men drinking and turns to the watchful figure next to him. "Is this the place?"

"Could be." Holton puts up his hand for quiet, motions forward and they creep closer. Through the low branches of the trees, they can see a man turn around and listen into the canyon. The two secreted observers hold their breath and watch. Holton puts his hand over the boy's eyes, tilts his head down and whispers quietly, "Don't look at 'em or he'll sense we're here."

The man in the camp stares into the brush, and Jules peeks over Holton's shielding hand to see the wound-crusted cheek of Bloody Ben Sighold. The young boy's mind floods with vengeful rage.

Jules grips the Walker pistol tight, grabs the fancy handled pistol from his belt and hisses low, "It's him!"

Holton quickly wraps his arms around Jules to restrain him. "Wait …"

They both watch quietly, as Bloody Ben finishes scanning the area and looks back to the Comanchero renegades settling into their drinking festivities for the evening. Ben touches his hand over fresh scratches at the back of his neck and ducks through the blanketed door of a small stone hut.

The mix of emotions and pent up anger nearly puts Jules on the edge of tears as he studies the hostile camp. "Where are my sisters?"

Holton looks to the boy with a remorseful seriousness. "There are about two dozen armed men in there. We have to be careful …"

The young man, bent on revenge, glares toward the camp with boiling, hate-filled eyes.

"I'll kill them all…"

"We need to have a better plan than that."

Jules blindly stares ahead and speaks aside to Holton. "You want to go get Bear and the others?" The boy looks edgy and his behavior is unsettling, as he holds the Walker and ivory-handled Colt at the ready.

Holton studies him a short moment and shakes his head. "I'm not going off to leave you here alone here, if that's what you're thinking."

"Do you have any better idea?"

The buckskin-clad tracker rests his rifle across his knee, watches the revelers moving around the camp and sighs, "The best thing to do is wait awhile."

"What about my sisters?"

"We don't even know they're here."

Jules stares at Holton and makes an effort to keep from crying. "You think they're dead, don't you?"

"If they are here, I know they will be killed if we charge in there without thinking first."

With a hesitant nod, Jules sits back on his heels, holds the Walker and fancy revolver in his lap and stares into the lively camp of mixed breed Indians and outlaws. Holton shifts quietly on his haunches and settles in for the uncertain wait.

~*~

Several large fires blaze around the encampment, as the sun slips behind the high canyon walls. The hostile mix of Comanchero gathers around the burning pyres while they drink, sing and shout into the night. Bloody Ben exits the stone hut and walks to one of the clusters of men. He receives a bottle from a lounging half-breed and takes a long, intoxicating swallow.

The fires make dark silhouettes of the drunken revelers, as Bloody Ben settles in amongst the others. In the grouping of men, Black Hand rises to his feet and flaunts fresh scalps amongst scattered fragments of a speech. Raucous whoops and singing commences, only to be interrupted intermittently by drunken calls into the coming night.

~*~

The light from the camp flickers through the shading branches of scrub and onto the two concealed onlookers. Holton watches every movement and holds his rifle, cocked and ready, across his lap. Jules' eyes continue to flash with a burning anger as he stares ahead at the murderous revelers. "I'm smaller and can sneak in to search those huts."

"When the drink has took hold, I'll go it alone."

The young man glances at Holton and stealthily picks up a small stone from near his foot. He tosses it into the brush and waits for his observant protector to turn his head away to listen. Jules holds the fancy, single-action Colt in one hand and his Walker pistol with the other as he prepares to bolt.

"The hell with that!" Darting from the brush, Jules scampers low across the dark ground to the nearest branch-fashioned shanty. Holton reaches out to stop him, but the determined youth is already gone. He watches as Jules sneaks around in the shadows near the closest wood structure.

The boy peeks in one of the windows and looks back to Holton shaking his head to the negative. Holton murmurs to himself as Jules continues on to the next cabin and inspects the interior.

"Dammit boy, be careful…"

Satisfied with the vacancy of the wood-constructed dwelling, Jules moves on to the stacked stone structure that Bloody Ben was seen exiting earlier.

From afar, Holton watches as Jules peeks through the window and seems to freeze in his tracks. Holton remains hidden in the brush as Jules looks back at him then slowly moves around to the front of the shack. The boy slowly pulls back the woven blanket door and slips inside.

Holton places his rifle stock to his shoulder as he whispers quietly, "No. Don't go inside … Dammit, kid." He eases his finger across the trigger on the big-loop rifle and puts the stone dwelling in his gun sights.

In the wavering darkness of evening, the concealing blanket covering the door remains idle and no movement can be seen within the structure. The Comanchero renegades continue their rowdy celebration as the firelight casts their outlines across the ground. Watching and waiting at the edge of the shadows, Holton sits alert to every movement and sound in the outlaw camp.

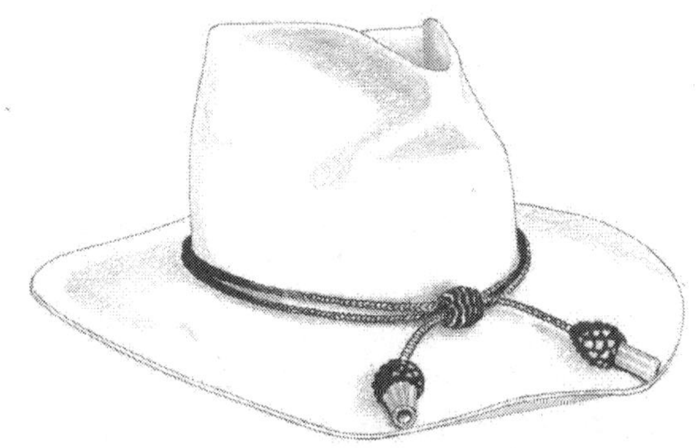

Chapter 33

The chill of daybreak hangs with a slight mist around the Comanchero camp in the deep, secluded canyon. Small wafts of smoke rise off the smoldering coal remains from the night's fires and hang in the air like hazy apparitions. A coughing grunt interrupts the quiet camp, and the casual groupings of slumbering renegades scattered on the ground, while most are still passed out before starting on the hang-over of a new day. Rays of sunlight peek over the cliff walls, as the morning light spreads across the canyon floor.

Bloody Ben Sighold sits up from his place on the ground and smooths back his long greasy hair. Grabbing a whiskey bottle from the ground, he takes the last remaining swallow and tosses it away. The unkempt man rises to his feet and stretches the morning kinks from his back. Ben scans his eyes around the sprawled, random figures then walks to the stone hut with the blanketed door and stands before it.

At the edge of the camp, concealed in the brush, Holton holds his cocked rifle firm to his shoulder. He stares down the barrel's blade sights to the back of Bloody Ben's greasy scalp. The rifle holds steady and Holton takes a deep decisive breath as he starts to squeeze his finger against the ready trigger. The clattering sound of several horses coming down the path from above catches both their attentions and Holton eases his finger away from taking the shot.

Bloody Ben shoots a suspicious glance over his shoulder toward the place where Holton conceals himself before turning to the incoming group of riders. Holton watches through the brush as the Mexican bandit, Poncho, leads Sergeant Kilbern and his group of US Cavalry troopers into the Comanchero camp. Ben steps away from the stone hut and walks to greet Poncho and the soldiers near the center of the encampment. The fresh, crusting scab on Ben's cheek oozes and cracks when he smiles up at the Mexican bandit.

"Well, hello there, Poncho. Who have you brought us here today?"

Sergeant Kilbern rides forward alongside Poncho and draws his pistol from his military flap holster. He holds the gun non-threateningly, but at the ready. The troopers cluster in a group behind him facing outward. Through the slight haze of mist and smoke, the sergeant scans the filthy renegade camp cautiously.

"We aren't looking for trouble with you people ... only the outlaw and wanted murderer, Holton Lang."

Bloody Ben stares up at the military riders and finally settles his gaze on Sergeant Kilbern. "I know the name but haven't made the acquaintance. A wanted outlaw and murderer, huh?"

Poncho licks the dusty fronts of his teeth and grins as he leans down on his saddle horn toward Ben. "The fringed buckskin man using the rifle with the boy at Fort Tularosa was 'im."

Bloody Ben reflects a moment and looks over his shoulder in Holton's general direction. "He may be around, but he ain't showed himself yet."

The small troop of US Cavalry begins to scan around the area nervously and move into more defensive positions, as various Comanchero start to rise from their drunken stupors. Bloody Ben watches as the commotion of the new arrivals attracts the camps attention. With weapons in hand, the Indian and mixed-blood renegades noticeably outnumber the soldiers, two to one, as they encircle the small assembly.

Bloody Ben smiles knowingly and offers a cordial gesture to Sergeant Kilbern. "You're welcome to wait awhile to see if he shows up."

The Sergeant looks around the hostile camp, recognizing the disadvantaged situation, then to Poncho, sternly. "Our deal, Sir, was for you to lead us to him."

Poncho continues to grin as he looks to Ben. "I did not know he would not be here among friends."

One of the Comanchero renegades steps forward and tosses Poncho a loaded revolver. The Mexican looks at the donated pistol amused, cocks it and waves it at Kilbern.

"You said this outlaw and murderer, Holton Lang was a vicious bandit … This is the place where they would be."

Sergeant Kilbern looks back at his men as they unfasten the flaps on their holsters, realizing the grave circumstances. Bloody Ben leisurely combs his fingers through his tangled hair and rests his hands atop of his head. He smiles at the soldiers as his eyes travel around to the superior number of outlaws surrounding them.

"Why don't you all be gracious guests, toss down your guns and wait for him?"

Poncho turns his horse to Kilbern and directs the aim of his pistol to chest level. The sergeant observes as the gun is pointed straight at him and stares livid at his former prisoner.

Poncho shrugs his shoulders in mock innocence. "Eh, soldier boy. I figure our deal is off."

A thick bead of perspiration forms up and travels down from Sergeant Kilbern's military hat. He clenches his jaw and makes a quick assessment of the devastating odds. Despite the cooler temperature of the canyon, an unrestrained flow of nervous sweat trickles down the officer's dirt-streaked cheek.

"Yes, our deal is off …"

Poncho laughs his distinct, sardonic cackle and uncocks the revolver in his hand. He rests the pistol against his leg and smiles down from horseback at Bloody Ben and the amassed crowd of armed outlaws.

"I brought you all something nice, eh?"

Kilbern raises his military revolver, cocks it and shoots Poncho square in the chest cavity. The Mexican clutches his breast and gives off a howling scream, as his horse begins to buck through the middle of camp. In a sudden explosion of activity, the mounted US Cavalry troopers engage in an exchange of gunfire against the overwhelming number of Comanchero renegades.

The camp begins to fill with clouds of gun-smoke, as every man unloads their firearm into the melee. Holton keeps his rifle firm to his shoulder as he levers and fires off several rounds. Taking aim at Bloody Ben, he shoots a missing shot as Poncho's horse goes bucking past. The crazed animal pushes Ben aside and the bandit leader ducks for cover.

Holton continues his barrage of gunfire on the camp as he hits a Comanchero reloading a rifle. Levering repeatedly, Holton methodically fires into the mixed crowd of outlaws. Tagged with hot bullet lead, the bandits go down, one at a time. Amidst the skirmish, several troopers are shot from horseback, as the others charge around haphazardly trying to control their mounts in the violent confusion of battle.

Burned black-powder smoke chokes the canyon with an acrid haze, while Holton remains in his shooting position at the edge of the camp. He levers the long gun, as another smoke-tinged shell casing is tossed out the top of his repeating rifle. He fires again, all the while keeping a sharp eye on the stone dwelling with the blanketed door.

Men with smoking guns scatter around the camp and shoot their firearms at assorted members of the engagement. Unmounted horses squeal and trot away from the violent confusion. Holton curses under his breath as the blanket entrance to the stone shack is tossed aside, and Jules steps out with the fancy Mexican pistol in hand.

The boy stands his ground in the doorway and fires off several shots at random outlaws as they flee for cover or grab at passing horses. A grease-painted warrior stumbles, then gets trampled by a cavalry mount, after receiving a gunshot wound from the young man. The camp is consumed in a whirl of spent gunpowder, shrieking horses and running men, as the report of pistols and rifles continues unabated.

Chapter 34

Standing outside the rock-stacked cabin with the blanket door fluttering behind him, Jules fires off a shot and hits on target. One handed, he easily cocks the hammer on the fancy, Mexican pistol and takes aim again. Around the corner of the shack comes another brigand and, suddenly, Jules is facing the shirtless chest of Bloody Ben Sighold.

The revolver barks instantaneously and Jules puts a close-range slug in the side of Ben who crumples with pain. Blood gushes from the fiery wound. Bent over, the outlaw puts his hand over the injury and looks directly at Jules with a shocked expression.

"You damned kid … You shot me again!"

Overwrought with rage, Bloody Ben pulls a long shimmering knife blade from his high-top leather boot and growls low, "I'm gonna skin you alive this time, boy … then those girls too."

Jules thumbs back the single-action hammer and pulls the trigger to an empty *click*. The towering man with a bullet wound in both his mouth and his gut stares down at the boy. Jules opens the side-loading gate on the pistol, turns the cylinder and starts to reload.

Fresh blood squeezes from the gunshot wound on his side as Ben grips it with his hand. "You are one hell of a funny kid to think I'm gonna let you toss more lead in that piece to shoot me with."

With his crimson-soaked hand, Bloody Ben grabs Jules by the shirt collar and poises his knife to slice into the boy. A whirling rifle bullet suddenly rips through Ben's forearm, shattering the bone, and the knife tumbles to the ground. Jules shakes free from Ben's grasp, as the wounded outlaw howls in pain. He looks over to see Holton rushing from cover and charging toward them while spin-cocking his rifle.

The injured outlaw cradles his useless arm near his abdomen wound and glimpses over at Jules. Filled with indignation, the young man crashes the short-barreled pistol against Ben's temple. The solid crack of gun steel on skull spins Bloody Ben Sighold to the ground and he lies motionless, as intermittent gunshots continue to erupt all around.

Holton rushes up and slides to a stop next to Jules. He raises the rifle, snaps off another shot and protectively tries to shield the boy from harm.

"Best be reloading that pistol, son. Where's that nine pound hog-leg yer fond of?"

Jules finishes ejecting the empty shell casings and pulls reload cartridges from the back of Holton's gun-belt. "My sisters are inside. I left the big Walker pistol with them."

Holton fires his rifle and levers it again. He glances down at Jules dropping another shiny, brass cartridge-load into the pistol cylinder and asks, "They still alive yet?"

"Mostly."

Shouldering the big-loop rifle, Holton fires toward a bandit and watches another trooper get gunned down in the mix. "We need to git 'em out and clear from here quick!" Holton fires again and cocks an empty rifle. He squats down and pulls fresh rounds from his almost empty gun-belt.

One of the Comanchero outlaws rushes toward them, and Jules takes aim over Holton's shoulder and fires. The warrior, in half-Indian garb, tumbles forward and writhes in pain from the gunshot. Jules cocks the pistol again and lines up a target. Holton steadily reloads the rifle and observes the losing battle of the outnumbered troopers.

"Them boys in blue ain't gonna last much longer."

Holton watches as Sergeant Kilbern, still horseback, pulls his sabre from his saddle rig and faces off against two Comanche warriors with tomahawks. He slashes away defensively until his wounded horse collapses, and he gets knocked to the ground. Holton levers his loaded rifle and shoots one of the hostile attackers, as Kilbern runs the other through with his cavalry sword.

Falling exhausted, to one knee, Kilbern looks toward Holton, hesitates then nods a thankful acknowledgment. Holton shoots at another renegade, as an Indian lance pierces Sergeant Kilbern's chest, dropping him back on the ground. As the boy takes another shot with the pistol, Holton lowers his rifle and calls to Jules, "We've lost here ... we got to git."

"I'll grab my sisters!"

Jules throws back the blanketed door when, suddenly, the attention-getting reverberations from an army worth of firing guns comes thundering down the trail from above. Whipping the wagon team at a breakneck downhill speed, Private Dedman steers wildly into the camp with Alice, skirt flying, holding on behind the backrest. Bear stands at the rear of the wagon box cranking rounds through a brand new tripod-assembled Gatling gun.

"Wahooey! Run for the hills 'n pucker yer hides, ya outlaw trash, 'cause I'm gonna tear you up!"

Bright brass-primed cartridges descend from the top-loading magazine tube and are cranked into the steadily revolving gun barrels. The spray of fired bullets tears into the outlaw camp, as powder-scorched shell casings drop into the bouncing wagon bed below. Coming along behind the four wheeled setup with the repeating gun, two Texas Rangers swoop in on horseback with pistols blazing in each hand.

On the trail of the outlaw Comanchero after their latest murder raid, Ranger Hobbs rides alongside Ranger Bentley. They tear onto the scene and shoot their dual pistols with deadly precision. In the revived skirmish, a pair of wounded soldiers crawls from the lively mounted horsemen's path. Hobbs breaks away to chase down a running renegade and clubs him with the long barrel of his handgun.

The other ranger's excited horse rears, and Bentley fires off a missed shot at a Comanchero starting to mount his pony. Hobbs watches the uninjured renegade get horseback and hollers at Bentley, "Hey ya cross-eyed, shootin' bastard … now he's taken to hoof and gonna get away!"

As his rearing animal comes down and does a jumping crow-hop, Bentley roars back at his ranger partner, "The hell he is …"

"There he goes, Bentley!"

"I'll get 'em, dammit!" Getting his horse under control, Ranger Bentley chases after the mounted hostile who flees down the canyon.

Holton watches the tide of opportunity quickly turn as the outlaw Comanchero effectively get gunned-down by the hail of bullets from the military, hand-cranked, revolving weapon. Private Dedman continues to circle the wagon, as Bear reloads the gravity-fed ammunition magazine.

The renewed eruption of fighting lasts only a few moments longer, before the few surviving hostiles throw down their weapons in surrender. Ranger Hobbs scampers his horse over next to the wagon and calls out as he motions to several surrendered hostiles, "You there, Bear-fella! Keep that hand-drive repeater on them four rascals while I re-stack my shooters."

The mounted ranger tucks one pistol in his wide, leather waist belt, as he reloads the other handgun. The renegades gawk at the occupied Ranger, walking alongside the wagon, and begin to make a move for the brush. Bear cranks the gun handle around and lets go a burst of gunfire near their feet until they step back into an obedient cluster.

Positioned behind the smoking set of gun barrels, Bear spits a steam of tobacco juice to the side of the mounted ranger. "I got 'em gathered, but they're yer geese to pluck."

Hobbs twirls a freshly loaded pistol and holsters it to begin with the other. "Much obliged."

Bear waves a salute and kicks a cluster of spent brass cartridge shells across the wooden bed of the wagon. "Makin' a ruckus is what I do best."

The ranger finishes reloading his other handgun and a grin appears under his long moustache. He waves gallantly. "And a fine brouhaha it was too." Ranger Hobbs touches his spurs to horse-hide and steers his mount toward the surrendered Comanchero.

The wagon rolls to a stop, and Private Dedman ties off the lines of the winded mule team on the brake handle. He helps Alice slide down from the wagon bench, and she rushes over to aid the wounded soldiers. Dedman follows her lead, and they place coverings over the deceased before carrying the wounded to the shelter of the military escort wagon.

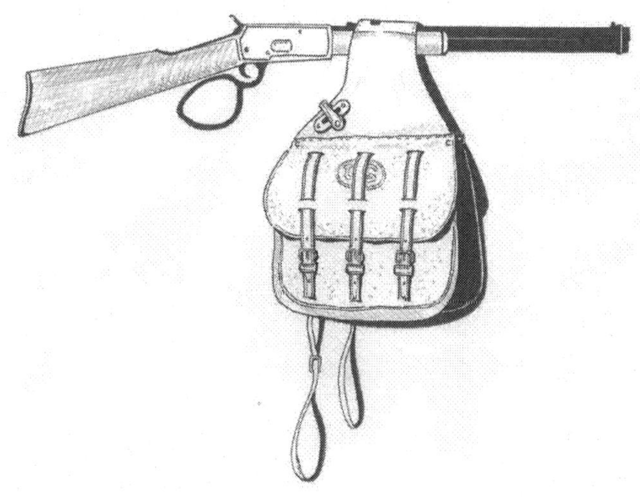

Chapter 35

The haze of expended gunpowder drifts through the canyon and filters through the broken sunlight around the embattled camp. Holton thumbs several more fresh cartridges into the side gate of his rifle and turns to Jules, asking, "You got any extra holes in ya, boy?"

"No Sir, but he does." Jules gestures to the ground where Bloody Ben Sighold was laying and discovers him gone. Only a faint trace of blood from his recent wounds remains. An empty feeling of dread comes over the boy as he stares at the vacant spot on the ground. With his pistol cocked and ready, Jules dashes around the corner of the cabin, searching for the body.

"He's gone!"

Holton racks the lever on the big-loop and scans his rifle's aim around the surrounding brush. His gaze strains to the depths of the undergrowth hoping to find any sign of the escaped outlaw.

The intuitive tracker studies the ground, his eyes following the blood trail, when the unexpected sound of a single gunshot is heard breaking the solemn stillness of camp. Holton spins around and quickly realizes the pistol shot came from inside the rock-stacked cabin. A cold wave of horrific shock passes over him as he stands motionless.

Jules comes running from around the corner of the stone shack and looks at Holton. He reaches for the blanket-covered door just as another explosive gunshot echoes through the quiet camp. The young man pulls back the blanketed entry and looks inside at the woeful carnage.

Nearly folding at his knees, Jules holds to the door frame of the cabin for support. The young man stares, with emotions shattered beyond comprehension, as he observes one sister shot directly in the heart and the other still holding the deadly weapon to her own mortal head wound. A faint gasp utters from his lips.

"Noo ..."

Jules looks to the oversized Walker pistol in the frail hands of his sister. Her small body falls limp and the large horse pistol tumbles to the ground. Consumed with despair, Jules stares at the firearm and the lifeless bodies of his remaining kin.

"You were safe now ... why?" With trembling lips, Jules stares in stunned disbelief.

Holton steps forward and puts his arm around the boy, holding him from crumpling to the ground.

"I'm sorry, son…"

"Why did she have to do that?"

"Sometimes the unfortunate things that happen to us in life are just too much to live with."

"I could have saved her."

Holton gives the young man's shoulders a slight squeeze. "You did save them."

Jules drops the fancy Mexican pistol and wraps his small arms around Holton. The young man puts his whole face into the worn buckskin shirt of the man embracing him and starts to weep uncontrollably. Holton leans down, holds the boy tightly and murmurs softly to him, "You can let it out … it's been a long time a' comin'."

Holton kneels and wraps Jules in a firm embrace, as the distraught youth lets his body convulse with sobs. He clutches the back of Jules' head to his chest and quietly whispers heartfelt condolences.

Across the camp, Alice stands over the wounded body of a soldier she was tending. She stares at the man and boy connected by heartache. Her womanly features fill with a motherly look of commiseration, as she watches Holton offer what little comfort he can to the grief-stricken boy.

~*~

A pair of tall, fancy-stitched riding boots with spurs is kicked up on a broken tree stump. From his lounged position, Ranger Hobbs gestures with his pistol at the group of Comanchero renegades, while they load and secure another dead cohort across the back of a pack-saddle pony. "Be sure to lash 'em tight now. I don't want limbs fallin' off or a' waggin' in the wind on the way to the capitol building in Austin."

One of the Comanchero gives the Texas Ranger a cross glance, and Hobbs leans forward with his pistol barrel raised. "I get another soured look from you like that, and I'll knock yer nose off."

The renegade sniffs and looks away as he speaks. "It will be a long trail for you, Ranger."

The spritely ranger leaps to his feet, steps forward and grabs a hold of the man's shirt sleeve. He quickly spins him around and jerks him close. The renegade sneers unpleasantly, and Hobbs pistol-whips him across the bridge of the nose. "Gonna be longer for you, nursin' a busted beak!"

The man howls in pain, as Ranger Hobbs pushes him aside and speaks to the other outlaw prisoners. "Let that be a good lesson to the rest of ya. Now git them others tied horseback, 'fore I lose my humor."

The sound of horse footfalls approaching in shallow water down-canyon catches the camp's attention. Shortly, Ranger Bentley appears in the small stream, leading a second mount. The poker-faced ranger waves a salute and looks back at his prisoner, bound astride with his hands in front on the saddle horn. The Comanchero bandit, clad in partial Indian costume, slumps over to ease the pain of a blood-smeared bullet wound through the leg.

Ranger Bentley rides up to Hobbs and halts his lathered and sweat-crusted mount. Ranger Hobbs grins widely as he looks over the wounded prisoner.

"Took ya long 'nough. Ya stop for a siesta?"

Bentley looks down and grimaces. "He was running fast for the Indian Nations."

"That why ya shot 'em in the leg?"

"Was aimin' for his horse."

Hobbs gives a sly, amused wink. "He's lucky he warn't shot in the head."

"Him or the horse?"

"Either."

Ranger Bentley looks around the ravaged camp and sees Bear helping Private Dedman with the wounded troopers near the back of the wagon. The deceased soldiers in uniform are wrapped in old blankets and laid out for transport home. Of the original group of troopers lead by Sergeant Kilbern out of Fort Tularosa, only three still catch breath, despite several wounds inflicted in the skirmish.

The distinct grind of a shovel crunching in the ground through rocks and sand catches the ranger's attention. He looks around and he sees Holton digging a short grave near the edge of the canyon under a low-slung oak tree. Ranger Bentley's gaze moves across the camp to Jules slumped before the rock shack with the blanket over the door. He watches as the young boy sits with his head down, staring at the ground.

Bentley shifts uneasy in the saddle and peers down at Hobbs. "What happened to the boy's sisters?"

Hobbs steps closer, speaking in a low, hushed whisper, "A terrible thing. One of 'em took the life of the other and then kilt herself."

Bentley removes his hat, looks to the boy and swallows hard. "He seen her do it?"

"Near 'nough."

The horseback ranger peers around the ravaged camp and takes in the morose scenery. He eyes the renegades loading the pack animals with the dead corpses and asks, "You got Ben Sighold in that bunch?"

Ranger Hobbs shakes his head negative. "That slippery bandit got away during the fight. Put that young boy in a tizzy when he couldn't find 'em.

Bentley replaces his flat-brimmed hat on his head and looks at the five dead bodies draped over horses and the dozen deceased Comanchero stacked nearby.

"What about them piled over yonder?"

Hobbs shrugs casually to the pile of bodies. "Cain't take 'em all or we'd have every wolf 'n coyot' in North Texas on our trail. I grabbed a few that I recognized 'n figured we'd bring 'em along for the Govern'r."

The observant Texas Ranger remains astride his horse and tosses the lead rope to the mount with his wounded prisoner over to Hobbs. Ranger Bentley looks approvingly over the surviving Comanchero renegades, including the one with the busted nose, still whimpering on the ground.

"Make sure you've pulled all their weapons 'n have 'em burn them others along with the whole camp."

Hobbs tilts his head agreeably and gives Bentley a friendly pat on the pants-leg. The mounted Texas Ranger wheels his horse away and rides across the camp toward Holton who continues digging the small grave.

Chapter 36

Under a strong and wide-spreading oak tree, Holton tosses another shovel-full of rocky ground aside from the grave. He steps clear of the hole and ducks from under the low branches when Ranger Bentley rides over. Dark stained patterns of sweat show on Holton's buckskin shirt as he looks up to the mounted Texas Ranger.

In the midday sun, Bentley, in his sloped heel and spurred, tall leather boots, looks to be a fine example of the renowned enforcement company. His ensemble is complete with tan, striped canvas britches, a loose sleeved cotton blouse and an encircled star badge pinned to his vest pocket. The ranger looks down mournfully at the shovel in Holton's hands, then over to the small grave.

Holton stands firm and stoic, with the shovel before him, while Bentley dismounts. The ranger stands about the same height as Holton and holds himself with a ramrod straight, upright posture.

After a quick glimpse over his shoulder toward the boy, Bentley leans closer and speaks low in reverence for the dead. "I heard what happened with the sisters."

A glistening of moisture develops across Holton's eyes, as he nods and glances toward Jules sitting at the stone shack with Dog nearby. He looks past the pair and watches Ranger Hobbs having the men stack loose brush over the dead renegade bodies. Bentley hesitates, then interrupts Holton's mournful gaze with uncomfortable conversation. "You gonna bury them gals here?"

Holton nods. "No place or kin to take 'em to."

The ranger nods and toes his boot on the ground before asking what's on his mind.

"What about the boy?"

Holton's look returns to Jules sitting near the cabin door, and his heart reaches out to him.

"Don't know yet."

Ranger Bentley follows Holton's gaze over at Jules and sighs, "Bear told us some about his situation. How old is he?"

Holton thinks a quiet moment then shakes his head. "Cain't tell 'xactly. He's a mite older now from doin' what he's done 'n seein' what he's seen."

Ranger Bentley crosses his arm across his chest and rests his other palm on the butt of his revolver.

"You think he'll try after Ben Sighold again?"

"Seein' as he followed him this far I don't imagine him quitin' anytime soon. Bloody Ben is shot up some, so his trail shouldn't be hard to track."

The ranger scans the surrounding underbrush and dark, shaded areas around the perimeter of the encampment. "Hell, he could be dead just outside the camp here." Holton stabs the shovel blade into the loose ground. "We'll find out soon 'nough."

The ranger pauses hesitantly, looks around the camp then candidly resumes with the probing inquiry that finally comes out. "You gonna keep that boy?"

"I promised to help him see it through."

Ranger Bentley nods. "And I suppose he will hold you to your word?"

"He will at that."

The frontier lawman drops his hand from his belt and peers over his shoulder to the dog and boy seated together. Ranger Bentley ponders a moment then asks the obvious question, "Then what?"

"That's up to him."

Over near the wagon, Bear catches Holton's attention and gestures toward the stone-constructed hut. Holton gives him a grave nod and pushes the shovel aside. He looks to the Texas Ranger and takes a step past him. "Excuse me. We have an unpleasant task to complete."

Private Dedman and Bear approach the piled rock structure once inhabited by Bloody Ben Sighold and his captives. They look down at Jules sitting at the threshold and pull the blanketed door aside. The men step to the interior darkness and reappear momentarily with two small, lithe figures wrapped in woolen cloth.

Jules looks up as they slowly carry his dead sisters over to the grave site. He wipes the back of his hand across an eye and reluctantly pulls himself to his feet. Jules witnesses the end of his search, as Bear and

Dedman gently place the swaddled forms in the ground, nestled next to each other.

From the gravesite, Holton watches as Jules goes inside the dark hut and comes out again with the large Walker pistol clutched to his chest. The boy walks over and stands despondently, looking down at the dual grave for his sisters. Kneeling down, Jules carefully places the large pistol across their swaddled bodies.

"Let the Almighty protect you where I can't..."

Tears start to stream down the boy's face, as Dog rises from his spot in the shade and walks over to the burial site. With the exception of Ranger Hobbs by the prisoners, Alice and the others gather around the grave and remain silent. Jules lets the tears roll down along his nose and drip from his rounded cheeks. He finally swipes his hand under his quivering chin and turns away. "I got no family now ... so, goodbye."

The young man takes a deep shaky breath, controls his weeping and walks away with his head bowed. They all watch, silently respectful at the loss of youthful innocence. Holton hands the shovel over to Private Dedman, and the mournful trooper begins the job of back-filling the grave.

Holton moves toward Jules, but hesitates when he sees Ranger Bentley follow after the boy. The tall lawman approaches, puts his strong hand to the boy's shoulder and gives it a kindly tap.

"Death is jest a part of life. It's a tough pill to swallow at times, but livin' life ain't easy either. You can choose your family by the ones you surround yerself with and what you do to protect 'em."

Jules looks back at Ranger Bentley and nods kindly, "Thank you, sir."

The ranger turns Jules around toward him and peers down at the young man from under his wide brim hat. "You're a fine lad with a lotta sand. You'd be more'n welcome to trail back with us to Austin."

Swallowing hard, Jules grits his teeth to keep from crying again and looks past the Texas Ranger to Holton, standing apart from the ones by the grave site. "I appreciate the offer, but I still got business to attend."

Bentley stares at the young man and witnesses his unyielding resolve. He stands before Jules and speaks plain. "The man you're searching for, Ben Sighold, has been Ranger business for quite a few years. We'll get 'em one day."

Jules considers his options then looks up at Ranger Bentley. "I'd rather get him sooner than later."

From afar, Holton watches as the Texas Ranger talks with the young man and he reflects on his personal responsibility and influence in the current situation. The haunting sound of shoveled dirt weighs on his conscience, and he turns away. Holton looks to the grave of the two deceased girls and then at his longtime friend Bear, standing alongside the rescued woman, Alice.

Private Dedman continues his task of burying the dead and pushes a handmade grave marker into the ground. Without a word of farewell, Holton takes up his rifle from its leaned position against a tree and walks to his saddled horse in the shade. Bear watches him curiously then follows.

Holton inspects his saddle and tack, as Bear walks up behind and inquisitively grunts, "Where you off to Holton?"

Holton peers over his shoulder at his old friend and speaks low. "I'm leaving."

"I see that. But, where ya going?"

The big-loop rifle slides into the leather saddle scabbard and Holton gives it a pat to seat it firm. "I'm finished here. Dedman can git them soldiers back to Fort Tularosa and the Rangers can take care of the rest."

Planting his feet far apart in a wide-legged stance, Bear hooks a thumb over his shoulder.

"What about the gal?"

Holton steals a fleeting glance toward Alice, then stares ahead a long moment. Painful memories of a past love-lost swell over him, and he breaks his gaze.

"Take her home."

"She ain't got a home ta speak of and to tell ya the truth, I think she was kinder hoping to git along with you."

Holton puts his foot in the saddle stirrup and mounts. "I won't be any good to anyone. Do me a favor and take her where she needs to go."

Bear nods and scratches his whiskers. "I can git her back to Santa Fe or Fort Tularosa I guess. What are you gonna tell the boy?"

Holton sits tall in the saddle, adjusts his age-worn cavalry hat and stares out to the scrub tangled terrain beyond the encampment.

"He needs to start a life … The one he's been living won't come ta much."

Bear holds his arms across his chest, takes a deep breath and sighs, "I know that tone. Guess there's no talkin' you out of it or changin' yer course?"

"Thanks, Bear. Been good seein' ya."

Holton shuffles the leather reins through his hand and prods his horse to a slow walk across the camp toward Jules.

Chapter 37

The once embattled Comanchero camp is serene, as the mule team on the military escort wagon sits idle and the prisoners wait in the shade near the string of corpse-burdened ponies. Holton rides up alongside Jules, standing near the stone hut, and looks down at him. He is at a loss for the right words and finally the young man speaks first.

"I'll go get a horse."

Jules steps away and Holton clears his throat before speaking. "You're not going with me."

The young man pauses, then turns and looks up at Holton with an obvious hurt in his tear-worn eyes. "You said you'd help me find him."

The horseback figure musters his resolve and stoically stares down at the boy, trying to conceal his fatherly admiration. "We found your sisters and that's the end of it."

Jules shakes his head. "It's not finished until I kill him for what he's done."

"He's hurt a lot of folks and will get his due. The best way to live with the loss is just go on with life."

Jules clenches his trembling jaw and looks around the bleak camp. He watches Private Dedman by the wagon and Bear talking with Alice near the gravesite. His gaze pauses on Ranger Bentley as he speaks with Hobbs by the prisoners.

"Well, go on then 'n quit. You done your good deed." Jules looks up at Holton and speaks coolly, "I ain't got any money reward for you, but I thank ya for your time."

Holton swallows the sting of the boy's hurtful words and looks off, past Jules. "Hunting a man ain't no way to raise a boy. Them Rangers have a job of it, so let them to it."

Jules stares hard at the horseback figure before him. "Goodbye, Mister Lang."

Holton winces at the painful parting and takes a last paternal glance at the youth.

"Good luck to you, son."

"You can keep it … I got no use fer it."

Holton holds back his readied mount and watches Dog standing faithfully at the boy's side. He exchanges a knowing look with the loyal canine then nods his heartfelt consent and rides ahead toward Ranger Bentley and the others.

Jules observes as the two men exchange a few short words before shaking hands in farewell. Standing alone, with a listless expression, Jules solemnly watches Holton ride off away from the outlaw camp. The lone horseback rider disappears along the running stream and into the surrounding brush of the canyon.

~*~

The nearly abandoned campsite is devoid of sociable activity, as the wagon is loaded and the strings of ranger-seized horses are assembled in a long pack train. Jules climbs into the saddle and looks over the littered encampment. Private Dedman clucks, and the wagon team lunges forward with the deceased soldiers braced behind in the cargo bed. Alice sits alongside Dedman, as the military wagon leads the remaining mounted troopers out of the canyon.

Jules rides over to Ranger Bentley, who talks with Bear as the old scout climbs aboard and settles horseback. The two men halt their conversation and observe the youngster with the fancy, single-action pistol tucked at his waist and the Mexican Sharps rifle positioned across his lap.

Bear scratches his grey, bearded cheek and spits aside. "You make up yer mind yet, boy?"

Jules turns his gaze over his shoulder and watches the military wagon and riders make their exit out of the canyon. "I ain't going back to where I already been. If it is agreeable, I would like to accompany you rangers awhile?"

Ranger Bentley nods and looks back at Hobbs, who shrugs. "We would be proud to have you along."

Bear gestures to the fancy pistol and rifle on Jules lap. "Ya expectin' trouble?"

"When it comes along, I'll be ready to meet it."

The horseback riders turn to observe as Ranger Hobbs lights a cloth-wrapped tree branch from the last remnants of a campfire. He rolls the burning torch in his hands to encircle the flames then walks to each wooden structure in the camp and sets them afire. The Ranger ends at the stone-stacked hut and touches the fiery torch to the limbs of the overhanging roof. Bentley nods his approval and starts forward with his convoy of horseback prisoners and lifeless captures.

Bear and Jules sit alongside each other watching the procession of requisitioned Indian ponies and the incineration of the renegade camp. The burly scout shifts in the saddle seat and glances at Jules as he clears his throat with a cough. "Gonna keep after that man, huh?"

"Figured I'd have a better shot at findin' him with the rangers than if I do it by myself."

Bear nods and tongues the wad of chaw in his cheek. "Ol' Holton may not have said, but he has had some hard life experience with the notion of vengeance. He'll be the first to tell ya it's an empty feelin' that never gets filled."

The boy checks his swell of emotions and tries to keep his lower lip from quivering. His thoughts return to Holton. "Mister Lang … he gone off and quit me."

"And he did it for your own good and well bein'."

Jules sits and contemplates while watching the torched flames grow and consume the dry, brittle outlaw dwellings. "I'll finish what I started out to do."

The heat from the fires and smoke of the burning structures starts to churn thick in the confined canyon. Ranger Hobbs tosses the flaming branch on the pile of corpses and climbs aboard his tethered mount. He gives a wave as he lopes past Bear and Jules on his way out of the hazy ravine. The breeze swirls the polluted air, and Bear takes up his reins as his mount starts to skitter and shy from the blazing heat.

"You're fortunate that you come out of this thing alive. Do your sisters 'n family proud. Chase life, not death."

The billows of smoke start to overwhelm them both, and Jules turns away with tears once again streaking the dirt on his cheeks. Jules kicks his boot heels and lets his horse leap into a loping gallop away. The smoke stirs in a following cloud behind the horseback youth, and Bear takes a last look to the flaming pyres before coming along behind.

~*~

The parade of military wagon, with soldiers followed by the Texas Rangers leading their bounty prize and prisoners, travels out of the smoke-filled canyon. The wheeled cart, with Private Dedman and Alice, splits off and travels to the west, while the rangers continue on with their party traveling south. Bear rides up next to Jules and thinks hard on something profound to say. He hooks his finger in his cheek and tosses a brown wad of used tobacco chaw aside.

"I ain't got the words for ya, kid." Bear reaches out to pat the young man on the shoulder. Dog trots up behind, while Bear observes the rangy canine following faithfully and shakes his head, amused.

"Good luck to ya then."

Jules nods and looks ahead to the ranger procession. "Thank you, sir."

"You're a smart kid. Use that head of yourn for something other than a hat rack and you'll be fine."

With a friendly wave, Jules prods his horse and rides off to follow the path of the Texas Rangers. Bear looks down at Dog, who lingers behind at his side and watches. "Go on, ya mangy mutt."

Dog looks up at Bear quizzically.

"Don't you be followin' me around, you cur hound." Bear rides off westward toward the military escort wagon headed to Fort Tularosa and glances back as Dog follows him. He shakes his head irritated and spits to the side.

~*~

Not far from the incinerated Comanchero outlaw camp in Palo Pinto country, Holton rides through thick underbrush and trees along the river bottom. In one of the canyons forking off from the Brazos River, he seems to be following an unmarked imperceptible trail. He lets his horse amble slowly and leans low, observing the details of the obscure tracks.

With his rifle across his lap, Holton breaks through the brush and comes to a burrowed-out cave along the bank of the stream. Staring back at him from the shadows, the dark eyes of Bloody Ben Sighold cower in the hollow. The two men of action are static a moment, as they stare coldly at each other.

Bloody Ben finally winces from the pain of his wounds. "Come to finish me off, have ya?"

"I ain't here to comfort you."

Ben coughs a bloody hack and holds his broken wrist to his swollen, gunshot abdomen. "That damned boy has done put a bullet through my gut."

"He would'a put another through yer black heart if given the chance."

Holton splashes his horse a few steps closer in the shallow trickle of water, and Bloody Ben growls in discomforted pain.

"That little shit was the death of me."

"Comeuppances have strange packages."

Ben heaves out an aggrieved sigh and scoots forward from the cave into the broken sunlight.

"Who was it come out on top back there?"

"Nothing for you to go back to."

Consumed in a fit of coughs, Ben groans as his body wretches. "You're that fella ... Holton Lang?" Ben hacks a mouthful of blood again and spits it aside as Holton watches without a word. Ben wipes his mouth and speaks angrily. "Always figured I'd come to an end a lot quicker than this ... Crawling through the river bottom like a wretched animal to get stoved-up in a cave ain't no way to go."

Holton adjusts the rifle on his lap and clicks the hammer back.

"Better'n you deserve."

Growling with contempt, Bloody Ben's eyes flash hostile with a last bit of fight. "Well, you can kill me now! Be sure to chop off my head so they knows that it's me yer turning in for the reward."

Holton stares across the short span at the pitiful dying form of the outlaw in the muddy cave. He momentarily contemplates on memories of unsatisfied revenge. "I won't be takin' no prize."

Ben glowers at Holton as the rider backs his horse away. "At least take my scalp you damned half-breed!"

Turning his horse upriver, Holton looks back at Ben in the cave and cracks an astute grin.

"That boy has his revenge."

Ben tries to stand, but crumbles back from the meager effort. "You damned, half-breed savage ... Come back here and finish me!"

Holton walks his horse down the shallow stream and cuts up the narrow embankment. He sits his mount, satisfied, as he rides away. The howls of Bloody Ben dying a slow painful death echo through the canyon walls below.

~*~

Holton rides toward the western horizon at an easy measured pace through rolling hills and canyon breaks into the afternoon sun.

The End...

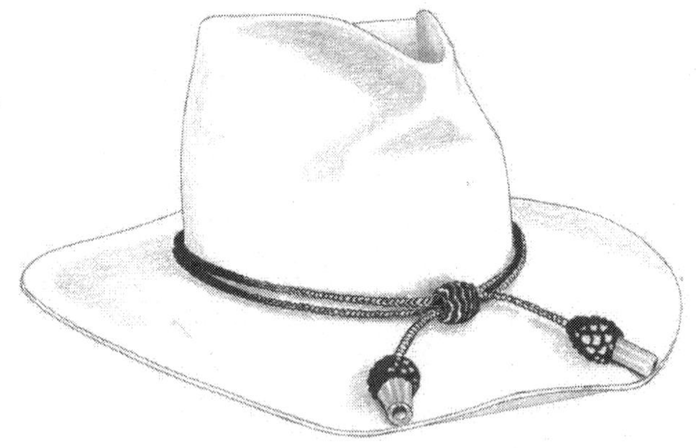

Eric H. Heisner is an award winning writer, actor and filmmaker. He is the author of several Western and Adventure novels: *West to Bravo, T. H. Elkman, Africa Tusk, Wings of the Pirate* and *Short Western Tales: Friend of the Devil*. He can be contacted at his website: www.leandogproductions.com

Al P. Bringas is a cowboy artist, actor and horse lover. He has done illustrations for novels: *West to Bravo, T. H. Elkman* and *Wings of the Pirate*. He lives and works in Pasadena, California.

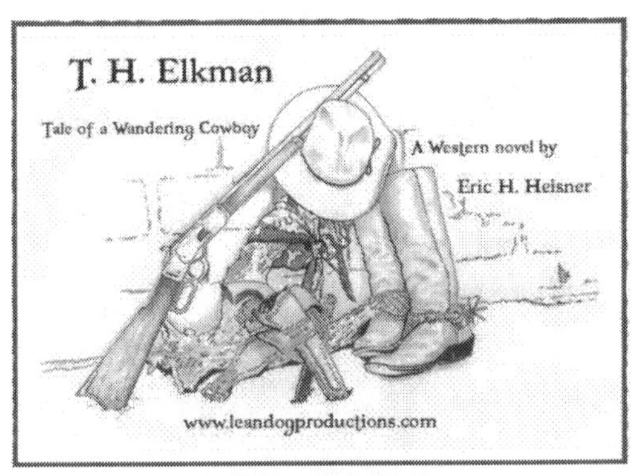
T. H. Elkman
Tale of a Wandering Cowboy
A Western novel by
Eric H. Heisner
www.leandogproductions.com

WEST TO BRAVO
A Western Novel
By Eric H. Heisner
WWW.LEANDOGPRODUCTIONS.COM

Wings of the Pirate
A high-flying Adventure Novel
By Eric H. Heisner
Limited time pre-order at:
www.inkshares.com
illustrations by
Al P. Bringas
www.leandogproductions.com

Made in the USA
Coppell, TX
23 March 2024

30452431R10146